KENT COAST OYSTER OBLITERATION

ALBERT SMITH'S CULINARY CAPERS RECIPE 11

STEVEN HIGGS

DEDICATION

This is book is dedicated to the current landlord of the Red Bull public house in Eccles.

The pub has occupied the same spot since 1675 and has doubtless endured many ups and downs over the centuries. My first visit was on a snowy day in 2011, stepping through the hallowed portal to be greeted by the enticing scent of an open fire. The low-ceilinged space was dimly lit, and my dachshunds fell asleep on my lap while I sipped a cold pint of ale.

The gentleman in question took over in the lockdown of 2020, using the enforced closure as an opportunity to completely renovate the aging decor. What was a slightly drab and dated interior, transformed under his leadership and vision into a tastefully modern environment.

All the tacky elements such as big screen televisions vanished, replaced by tables and chairs to create intimate cubbies where couples and families could sit and interact. The garden was completely reworked, and the man did almost all of it himself. I know this because I watched with keen interest over my garden wall. Drawn by the curious sound of power tools, I would abandon my writing to investigate, exchanging a few words and offering the landlord without customers a few moments of respite from his labours.

I now find an almost magnetic pull to stop in whenever I walk by.

To Timothy Gough. Sir, I salute you.

PROLOGUE

TANYA AND BALDWIN

Baldwin watched Tanya zipping up her knee-high boots. She was bent at the waist with her left foot resting on the stool set in front of the dressing table. Her right boot was already on, the two-inch heel doing wonderful things to the shape of her leg as he traced the curve upwards to her …

"Close your mouth, Baldwin." Tanya hadn't bothered to look up – she didn't need to. She had been shackled with the oaf of an idiot, posing as his wife, for almost a month now and had grown tired of his attempts to seduce her. To be fair to him, the cheesy lines and stupid, schoolboy efforts to impress her had diminished, but his need to stare at her and 'accidentally' catch her in a state of undress were as frequent as ever.

She already planned to leave him in a shallow grave. Actually, she was beginning to question why she hadn't already done so. The earl would find a replacement easily enough – the money he offered was the highest she had ever earned, though the job was also about the weirdest she'd encountered to date.

Baldwin looked away, snapping his lips together with a wince. He just couldn't understand why she continued to resist him. They were attractive adults in the prime of their lives and had been sleeping in the same bed for weeks as they travelled around the country performing the earl's strange requests.

Surely Tanya ought to want to have a little adult fun with him, even if it was just recreational.

"Are you ready?" she asked, straightening up and checking her pockets to make sure she had all she needed. They were posing as a married couple visiting the area for a wine-tasting getaway. They had several tasks to perform – none of which involved actually tasting wine though they had visited a vineyard.

Staying at a dreary bed and breakfast in Whitstable, Tanya wanted nothing more than to get the job done and leave. Yet they were destined to be stuck here longer than originally intended because Baldwin allowed the wine expert to escape.

He slipped Baldwin's grip, ran, climbed, and fell to his death. The earl had gone nuts, and knowing he would, Tanya had insisted Baldwin make the call for once.

Earl Bacon had been very specific about who he wanted them to collect – he always said *collect* and not *kidnap*. It was a wine connoisseur by the name of Simon Major. He worked for Chapel Hill, a wine label of some note and reputed to be among the best in the country.

They needed him, some of his award-winning vines, and a handful of workers from the vineyard to establish the earl's crop. They also stole two thousand cases of the earl's favourite wines, loading them, the workers, and the freshly excavated vines into a curtain-sided trailer before more of the earl's employees took it all away.

The connoisseur was the last piece of the puzzle. He was needed, the earl assured them, because only his refined palette would get the finished product to the right standard. The earl intended to have wine for the rest of his life and two thousand cases wouldn't see him through in his opinion.

Tanya didn't think the morbidly obese member of the gentry would live long enough for the vines they'd taken to produce their first crop, but whether he did or not had no impact on what she had planned for today.

They were in Kent and could not move on until they had completed all the tasks on their list. The earl wanted oysters and he wanted sausages. It was one of the strange vagaries about the titled fool that he was so specific about the food. It had to be this cheese from this particular dairy in Shropshire, or this vinegar from a tiny producer on the coast in Yorkshire.

Tanya put no thought to it – it was just a job, but Baldwin … Baldwin was beginning to annoy her.

Baldwin made a show of rippling his shoulders as he put on his jacket – he wanted to remind her just how broad and muscular they were. He performed press ups and other exercises every night before bed just to demonstrate his physical athleticism – and he did it in his underwear.

"Are you ready?" she repeated, hooking her handbag over one shoulder, and moving to the room's door to wait for him.

Giving up with a sigh, Baldwin said, "Yes, Tanya."

"Suzie," she corrected him with an annoyed and frustrated growl. "How hard is it to remember to stay in character? My name is Suzie Davis. You are Nathan Davis. We are accountants taking a short break for our tenth wedding anniversary."

He was going to give them away at some point. She was amazed he hadn't already. Next time, she was going to insist the earl teamed her up with another woman. She wasn't a lesbian, but that was the whole point. Two women could pretend to be, and having removed all the unnecessary sexual nonsense Baldwin introduced, they could focus on their work.

Baldwin muttered under his breath, berating himself for another slip up. If she would just get on board with the husband and wife act and sleep with him, he might be able to concentrate on something other than getting her clothes off. In his mind it was a simple and obvious solution.

One he'd proposed more than once, in fact.

Sensing now was not the time to raise the subject again, he checked his own pockets and nodded.

While she ran through options for how she might 'accidentally' kill him, Tanya opened the door and made her way to the stairs.

Dropping into her act, she called out loudly enough that the B&B owners might hear.

"Did you get the key, darling?"

Baldwin grumpily played along, dangling the chunky plastic fob with its two keys from his right hand and giving it a jingle.

"Yes, dear."

1

THE VINEYARD

Albert stepped out of the taxi and into a shallow puddle, his sturdy shoes displacing the water to leave a boot print in the thin layer of soft mud coating the road.

Rex padded across the back seat and out to join his human in the street. They were at the end of McKenders Lane in a small village called Eccles. Albert had never heard of it despite his own house being less than five miles from the spot on which he now stood.

Ahead of him was a vineyard.

The taxi driver leaned out of his window. "That'll be thirty-five quid, mate."

Albert withdrew his wallet and counted out four crisp ten pound notes, handing them over and stepping off to indicate no change was required. He thought the service was expensive, but no more so here than anywhere else in the country. He could have taken public transport, but there was no easy route from A to B and he was in a hurry.

Rex sniffed the air, sorting and categorising the scents caught in his powerful nose. A child had walked by less than an hour ago with an open packed lunch box – Rex could smell cheese and pickle sandwiches and a slice of mum's home-made cake. It had to be a kid because there was a sort of sticky, scruffy odour that went with the lunch smell.

There were horses nearby, and sheep somewhere too. Lots of dogs had been through – it was a regular dog walking route, Rex's nose assured him. Rabbits, badgers, and numerous other wild animals lived in the fields to his front, their scents as individually identifiable as colours to his nose.

Albert clicked his tongue.

"Come along, Rex. Let's see what there is to see."

The duo of elderly man and oversized German Shepherd dog had been away from their home county for weeks. Touring the British Isles to taste some of its most famous dishes and, where possible, learn how to make them, Albert had only returned now because an intriguing crime had very recently taken place.

During his travels, he'd come to believe there was a person orchestrating a sinister series of kidnappings and thefts. He and Rex first stumbled upon the mystery in the village of Stilton when they met a man employed to steal an entire shipment of the famous cheese. From there they inadvertently stumbled across two men sent to kidnap the Bedfordshire Clanger master baker.

The kidnappers ended up dead though Albert took no responsibility for what befell them. However, the events in the Bedfordshire town of Biggleswade convinced Albert that he wasn't imagining things – there really was someone kidnapping chefs and stealing both food and the equipment to make it. Needing a name to use as a term of reference, Albert called the unseen figure 'the Gastrothief'.

With that belief locked firmly in his head, he began tracking what he believed was a pattern of crimes, but it wasn't long before the trail went cold. He'd all but given up when his eldest son, Gary, a detective superintendent with the Metropolitan Police in London, contacted him to say there had been an incident at a vineyard in Kent.

So here he was, back home and set to investigate. He had no imperative to solve the case, but he believed the focus it required was helping to keep his mind strong. At seventy-eight, he had no idea how many years he had left and was glad to fall into bed each night believing he had done something worthwhile with his day.

Rex wasn't thinking in terms of master villains – such concepts were beyond him, but he could figure out when a crime had been committed and track the clues to root out the human behind it far faster than his human could ever imagine. That humans continued to rely on their eyes instead of their noses would forever annoy him, but he had come to accept his human's weakness as a trait of the species. The old man made up for it in other ways and was a reasonable sidekick most of the time.

By listening to the conversation between his human and his human's pup in the car yesterday – Gary had come to fetch his dad from Blackpool - Rex had learned that they were to investigate a suspicious death. In his human's opinion, it was probably a kidnapping gone wrong and that was almost the same as murder. Quite why humans felt the need to kill each other so regularly Rex could not comprehend.

He sniffed the air again, leaning into the slight breeze and closing his eyes as he searched for the cloying stench of blood. He could find no trace of it and his human was walking ahead, either choosing not to clip Rex to his lead or forgetting to do so.

Rex was happy either way, eagerly bounding past his human and through a gap in the fence line to access the fields beyond.

Albert followed at a brisk pace, marvelling at the view - who would have known it was so lovely here? A south-facing slope to his left was coated in neat lines of vines from the top of the gradient where it met the sky to a point on his right where it faded into the distance.

Too late in the season for there to be any greenery, the vines were devoid of leaves, the denuded stumps looking almost dead though Albert was certain they would burst into life again in the spring.

He had an appointment, courtesy of Gary's influence and connections, with the owner of the wine label. The buildings where they made and stored the wine were accessible by road, but Albert had chosen a different approach so he could get a sense of the area without anyone influencing where he went and what he saw.

A man had died after falling from a high shelf inside one of the vineyard's wine stores. That in itself wasn't necessarily suspicious, though it begged the question of why he had gone up there in the first place.

Simon Major, a wine connoisseur of some note and the man running the vineyard, had no good reason to climb the shelves. It prompted Albert to theorise that he was trying to get away from someone. It might have sounded like a wild guess, but four workers from the vineyard were missing, hundreds of cases of wine had been stolen, and some of the vines had been ripped up. It was this additional detail that tipped off Albert's son, Gary, and ultimately led Albert to want to investigate.

No one else would have reached the same conclusion, but Albert was certain the four missing workers had been kidnapped and the man who fell to his death had done so while attempting to evade capture. That the dead man was a wine expert sealed the deal so far as Albert was concerned – he fit the pattern of food specialists that had been vanishing all over the nation.

Were it not for his children, all three of them senior detectives in the Met, Albert felt quite certain he would be trying to figure this all out on his own. Instead, despite some early barriers he'd needed to erode, his children were all on his side. They believed in his theory of a 'Gastrothief' and were supporting his efforts to figure out who it was.

Half a mile into the fields, Albert reached the edge of a fence line and the start of the row of vines. He'd been able to see them through the window of the taxi when it took a road into the village that passed above the vineyard. The damage hadn't been visible then, but he could see it now away to his right.

An entire row of vines was missing, the ground where they had recently stood now looking like the plants had been torn from it.

Albert led Rex that way, his dog happily running free in the open countryside.

Rex sniffed as he went, revelling in the abundance of countryside in which he found himself. There were buildings in the distance and houses to his rear where they exited the taxi. Other than that, there was greenery in every direction.

He tried to mark it all and stopped at a handy puddle to refuel.

The air carried almost too many interesting scents. They were here to investigate a crime, he understood that, but there were very few human smells around. Those he detected were from passing dogwalkers his nose assured him - each accompanied by the scent of a dog.

Tracking a badger – purely out of interest – he kept his nose to the ground and let it guide him.

"Rex!" Albert called to turn his dog around before he vanished into some bushes. He had inspected the ground where the vines were removed, noting the presence of tyre tractor marks but reading little into it.

The marks could be hours or weeks old – it had rained yesterday, and the ground was still damp. There were puddles dotted here and there and mud where the frequency of people through some spots had churned the earth into a quagmire.

Pushing on, Albert struck out for the vineyard buildings. He had seen what there was to see in the vineyard and now it was time to ask some questions.

It was an uphill slog for the next five minutes, Albert's legs getting a workout, but not to the extent that he would regret it later. Rex was clearly enjoying himself, constantly darting back and forth, side to side as they made their way up the hill.

Just before they made it to the crest, the sound of farmyard machinery in the distance reached Albert's ears. A moment later, a field of sheep came into view along with a tractor trundling along the edge of a hedgerow half a mile away.

Rex could already smell that they were coming closer to sheep and horses, the heavy scent they gave off unavoidable.

They were spotted by people inside the buildings of the wine label, but ignored as just another man and dog out walking in the countryside until they rounded the buildings and came up the driveway.

Albert passed under a large, colourful sign boasting 'Chapel Hill Wines'. The picture beneath the title was of two bottles of chilled wine and a pair of glasses in the sunshine.

It clearly wasn't taken today, thought Albert, hoping he would get to go inside soon. The cool air was starting to seep through his clothes and boots. If Rex thought it was cold, Albert couldn't tell - his dog was still bounding around with seemingly limitless energy.

Rex was paying no attention to the cool air or to the dirty puddle water now dripping from the underside of his coat. Mostly, he was too busy following a scent. This time it was blood. Human blood and it was coming from dead ahead in one of the buildings. There wasn't much of it, only a trace amount really, but his nose was attuned enough to detect it, nevertheless.

He paused, waiting for his human to catch up when the old man called for him to stop, and checked they were ready to move on once the lead was clipped to his collar.

Intending to send the old man away since he clearly had no business at the vineyard, Adam Hodgson, the business owner's husband, moved to intercept him at the gate.

"Sorry, this is private property," he called out, expecting that would be enough to turn the old man around. When man and dog just kept on coming, Adam's features darkened. They'd suffered a terrible attack, losing a huge quantity of their product. Insurance would pay for it, but it impacted their market position and forced their customers to go elsewhere for their supply.

Adam believed the missing workers had stolen the wine and the vines and that Simon Major, a man he distrusted right from the start because he was far too good looking and got on far too well with Adam's wife, was behind the whole thing. Not that he'd formed that opinion himself. He got it from the chief inspector who'd visited the scene.

Simon Major had been found dead, the coroner confirming that he'd broken his neck when he fell. Quite what he was doing up there no one could fathom, but Adam remained convinced he'd figured it out: the other four had chosen to cut him out of the deal and had thrown him from the shelves while they were stealing the wine.

The chief inspector – Adam racked his brain, but couldn't come up with the man's name - said there were bruises on his body to suggest he'd been fighting back against someone. They were treating his death as suspicious, but hadn't yet labelled it as murder.

The reporters had arrived within hours. Like vultures circling above a wounded beast, they wanted to know what had happened, but equally they were digging for a story about whether the vineyard could survive. Their suppliers were going to have to get their wine from someone else – would they come back to Chapel Hill once they had grown more grapes the next year? What about the loss of Simon Major? Wasn't he the key behind their success as an emerging wine label?

Now there was an old man seeking to poke his nose in. Well, he was about to get the sharp end of Adam's temper.

"Mr Smith?"

Adam twisted at the waist, spinning around when his wife called out. She was hanging out of the door to the press room and waving to the old man.

Seeing her look his way, Adam was surprised when his wife shouted, "That's Mr Smith. I'm expecting him, darling. Remember I told you he was coming this morning?"

Adam didn't remember, though he was vaguely aware his wife had been telling him something about a private investigation and a senior detective from the Metropolitan Police who had contacted her. What that had to do with the old codger walking toward him Adam had no idea.

Albert extended his hand. "Albert Smith. I believe I'm expect-ed," he said with a smile, echoing what the lady had just said.

His features still guarded, Adam accepted the handshake, but only for the briefest of moments, barely allowing their skin to make contact before he withdrew his hand again.

"You'd better follow me then."

Albert expected the man to introduce himself and was surprised when he rudely turned away. It wasn't enough that the man had one of the weakest handshakes Albert had ever encountered, he had no manners to boot.

Rex, oblivious to such things, was attempting to pinpoint the location of a dog he could smell.

Doberman, he concluded, sampling the air once more as his human started to follow a man who appeared to have been waiting for them. The dog in question was here, or had been until very recently, but though Rex could smell him, of the dog there was no sign.

Curious to see what there was to find, man and dog followed Adam inside the press room.

2

THE KEY

U nlike her husband, Shelly Hodgson was as forthcoming as she could be, but it didn't take Albert long to conclude there wasn't much to learn from her. Like the previous victims he'd met, the Hodgsons just didn't know anything.

They had been targeted in a strange and seemingly random crime that baffled local police. There was little evidence left behind by the perpetrators and no one saw anything. Those who might have were missing.

Albert didn't want to come across as a nutter, so avoided mentioning the Gastrothief at any point.

While the humans talked, Rex waited. He listened, but didn't pay much attention – it was just words and words don't have a scent. Bored, he laid himself on the concrete, stretching out and closing his eyes. Only when he caught the smell of the Doberman again did he lift his head.

Albert had unclipped his lead and instructed him to stay as the other humans were showing where the police estimated Simon Major was when he fell. Untethered, Rex stole a glance in their direction to make sure they were not looking, then swiftly slunk in the opposite direction, nudging the door open with his head.

The instant he got his face outside, he spotted the dog.

"Hey!" he called out to get the Doberman's attention, but didn't want to bark loudly for fear it would draw the humans.

The large but lean, black and tan dog turned to see who was calling, and then curled his lip in warning.

"Calm down," Rex whined. "I'm not invading your territory, I'm just passing through. I'm here with my human to investigate what happened the other day when the human was killed."

The Doberman narrowed his eyes, his hackles still up as he warily watched the German Shepherd coming his way.

"So you're a what? A police dog or something?"

Rex went with it. "Yes. Something like that. I used to be anyway. Are you resident here?" he asked unnecessarily – the place stank of the Doberman's scent to leave no question this was his place.

"Is your nose not working right? I've marked every inch of this place."

Rex wanted to roll his eyes, but the Doberman was surly enough already.

"Just making conversation. Listen, if this is your place, you must have caught the scent of the new people who came here. The ones who were here when the human died the other night couldn't have done so without leaving their odour behind."

"Obviously," growled the Doberman. "And? You think I have some magical way of capturing it so you can smell it now? It was two days ago, there's nothing left of it. What little had lingered got washed away by the rain."

Rex had hoped a resident dog might be able to provide some insight, but the Doberman showed no inclination to do so.

"Rex!" Rex twisted his head around at the sound of his human's voice. The old man was emerging from the building they'd been in. He had the lead in his hand and was clearly expecting Rex to come to him, not the other way around.

Rex wanted to find a way to convince the Doberman to tell him something worthwhile, but doubted that was going to happen. Without bothering to give the dog another look, Rex walked back to

Albert, holding still while the old man clipped the lead onto his collar.

"Well done for not wandering off, Rex. I was worried you'd found the scent of a rabbit and gone to chase it."

Rex screwed up his face. "Found the scent of a rabbit? Are you nuts? The whole place stinks like rabbits. They are everywhere. Plus mice and rats, voles, badgers, foxes … it's the countryside," Rex replied with a sad shake of his head. If his nose worked like a human's, he doubted he would ever manage to get off his bed – the depression would be too crushing.

Albert had struck out. Well mostly, he considered. His visit hadn't been without gain. The operation had been slick, further convincing him that this was the Gastrothief at work. Neither Shelley nor Adam could recall seeing anyone unexpected at the vineyard or the surrounding area in the last few weeks, nor had there been any visitors who came by without good reason.

Simon Major was very well known in the wine-making community and respected for what he'd been able to achieve. When Shelley spoke about Simon, her husband, Adam, grumbled that they paid him too much and mumbled about being able to determine a good grape from a bad one himself.

Shelley ignored him, giving Albert the impression the argument was an old one she had grown bored of hearing. He considered, just briefly, that Adam Hodgson might have motive for wanting Simon Major out of the picture. However, he dismissed the notion no sooner than it arose – Adam Hodgson didn't possess the gumption to pull off the crime.

Albert thanked Shelley for her candid answers – they were facing a tough future at the business and there was nothing to be gained from giving an old man her time. Even if he caught the people behind it, and was somehow able to return the wine, the vines, and the workers, they would still be without their key person. Shelley made it quite clear their success was down to Simon Major's palate and knowledge.

Making his way back to where the taxi had dropped them off –

he had spotted a pub at the corner of the road when they turned in, Albert left the vineyard buildings behind. It would take half an hour to retrace their steps and that would make it a little after noon - the perfect time to break for lunch.

On the way, Albert thought hard about his next step. On the face of it there was no evidence trail to follow. Simon Major's death was considered to be suspicious, but that was a long way from labelling it a murder, so the local police would not be pursuing it with a great deal of effort.

Four people had vanished and that was also suspicious, yet according to Mrs Hodgson, the Chief Inspector who led the investigation was of the opinion that the theft of wine and vines was more likely to be an inside job and their disappearance all but confirmed it. His name was Quinn and Albert knew the family name if not the man himself.

There had been a Quinn in the Kent police during Albert's time on the force. Albert figured the man in question now was most likely the grandson of the one he knew all those years ago. Families were like that. His was for sure.

Shelley claimed Chief Inspector Quinn made no mention of kidnap – he was not concerned for the safety of the four missing workers, only their whereabouts. He wanted his officers to track them down and bring the case to a swift conclusion by catching them as they attempted to sell the wine to a third party. Albert felt certain their efforts would be focused on the ports. Being so close to Dover and the link to the European mainland, stealing the wine and getting it out of the country was an obvious move.

Albert could not fault the chief inspector, but he had an alternative theory. The concept of the Gastrothief was still one being discussed in quiet by a select handful of officers. Beyond his own children, there were perhaps half a dozen other persons aware of the off-the-books investigation.

Albert was the only person actively pursuing it and that was for the simple reason that it was so outlandish. A master criminal managing an empire of operatives sneaking about to steal food and kidnap chefs and food experts? Bonkers.

Until Albert had concrete, irrefutable evidence, not even his eldest son, Gary, a detective superintendent in his own right, was going to openly declare such a person existed. Albert knew he was lucky to have his children helping at all.

Free from his leash and able to roam, Rex snuffled along the ground once more, joyously following his own scent back to the gap in the fence where they entered the field. He paused at the edge of the road, waiting for his human to catch up.

The smell of a public house drifted through the air carried by the breeze. Too intangible for a human nose to detect, Rex could discern the smell of frying fish, the heady odour of ales, and the unmistakable aroma of a wood fire. He knew his human well enough to be certain that was where they were heading.

It suited him just fine. He was always ready to eat.

Albert clipped Rex's lead to his collar in an absent-minded way, his head too full of thoughts about the Gastrothief to permit anything else to enter.

Simon Major – his death was the key. Albert had been thinking about it since last night. Why had the Gastrothief targeted this particular vineyard? Kent was well-known for growing wine; the vineyards of Albert's home county won many awards and challenged the French, who were, to be fair, growing the same grapes in the same soil at the same latitude just a few miles away. Heck it was so close that people could swim there.

So to Albert's mind the one thing that set this vineyard apart was Simon Major. He was the reason for their success. Even the owner said as much. The Gastrothief didn't get him though. Simon died and that left the Gastrothief without the person he needed.

In Cumberland the sausage factory was raided for equipment and an award-winning sausage maker. Here they took vines and equipment for making wine, but what good were they without the man to make it all work?

Reaching the end of the road and strolling across the pub carpark, Albert knew what he was going to do next: he was going to find out who was considered to be second best. If the Gastrothief couldn't have Simon Major, then he was going to send his people to grab someone else.

At the door to the pub, Albert stopped. Rex had come to a halt and was sniffing the air.

3

CANINE STANDOFF

With a tug to get Rex moving, Albert pushed his way through the door and looked around. There was a meagre lunchtime crowd; a dozen customers dotted about inside. He doffed his hat, nodded with a smile to the clientele in general and made his way to the bar.

Rex came through the door behind his human, sniffing the air to confirm what he knew and using his eyes to find the resident dog.

A small Dachshund looked up from her perch on a comfortable couch in the corner of the bar by an open fire. She was lying on a rabbit hide and against the thigh of a man in his forties. The Dachshund's human had a trim beard speckled with grey that extended into his hairline, and a look of concentration focused entirely on his laptop computer.

As Rex followed Albert to the bar, the Dachshund plopped off the couch unnoticed by her human. She emerged from under a chair a moment later, sniffing the air to get a better sense of the new dog.

"I've not seen you in here before," she observed. "And you smell like Thor. You've just been to the vineyard then."

Rex's eyebrows waggled for a moment as he deciphered her meaning.

"Thor is the Doberman?"

"Yes. He's such a sweetie. He's in here all the time. I'm Millie."

"Rex," replied Rex, silently questioning her opinion of the surly dog he'd met. He'd struck out getting anything from Thor, but maybe the tiny sausage dog knew something. "I'm here investigating a murder. Possible murder," he corrected himself. "Did you hear about the human who died at the vineyard two days ago?"

"Ooh, yes! Thor was in here yesterday telling everyone about it. He said there were new people at the vineyard and the police have got it completely wrong."

Rex's ears were about as pricked up as they could get. The Doberman had given him nothing of use, but now the little Dachshund was telling him exactly what he wanted to know.

"Go on," he encouraged.

Millie wagged her tail, pleased to have someone who wanted to listen.

Albert was at the bar, paying for his drink and collecting a menu. The young woman serving him advised he should sit wherever he fancied. It gave him a range of options, each of which was equal to the others. The prime spot appeared to be the one by the fire. Sadly, that was taken, but as his eyes roved, he spotted a glass jar sitting at the end of the bar.

It was filled with bone-shaped dog biscuits.

Deciding that would be a more nutritionally balanced option than the bag of pork scratchings he'd already purchased for Rex, Albert looked down to ask his dog's opinion.

"Oh, you've found a friend," Albert observed, ruffling the fur between Rex's ears. When Rex glanced his way, Albert asked, "Would you like a biscuit?"

Rex didn't think the question required an answer since his response was predictable enough. Instead, he tried to explain what he was learning.

"There were humans at the vineyard. Two of them. A man and a woman. I'm going to see what else I can learn, but that stuff they told you about the police thinking it was an inside job? Utter codswallop."

Albert patted Rex's head. "Good boy. I shall take that as a yes."

Rex rolled his eyes and with a sigh went back to his conversation with Millie. He got interrupted before he could speak. Not once, but twice.

Firstly, his human leaned over to address Millie.

"Is that your owner sitting by the fire? It seems unfair to give Rex a biscuit and have you watch him eat it."

Rex heard the old man address Millie's human, interrupting the man as he worked on his computer. He didn't need to hear what was said to understand what was passing between the two humans, but could not have concentrated on it even if he wanted to because the pub door opened, and Thor's head came through it.

"You?" snarled Thor. "What are you doing here?"

That his question was aimed at Rex needed no explanation. Rex had tolerated the Doberman's attitude when he was on the other dog's turf. This was a public house though and either to be considered neutral territory, or at worst the property of Millie the Dachshund since she would have marked it.

Getting to his feet, Rex shifted around to face the Doberman who was now inside the pub. His human, the man from the vineyard, was coming through the door behind him.

Rex bared his teeth. "I'm tired of your attitude."

Millie jumped between the two much larger dogs.

"Whoa, fellas. This is my place. You'll behave nicely or I'll bar you both."

Albert hauled Rex back a foot, Adam Hodgson doing likewise with Thor.

"But I'm in here all the time," snarled Thor.

Millie wasn't about to be cowed just because the Doberman was twenty times her size and weight.

Getting in his face she growled. "Then you should know well enough to behave in my establishment, Thor."

Suddenly buoyed aloft as her human stepped in to scoop her,

Millie snapped a closing comment that turned the air blue and startled both larger dogs.

"Is she always that feisty?" asked Rex.

Thor was still staring up at Millie when he heard Rex ask the question.

"Yes." He flicked his head to expose the underside of his left ear. "See that scar? That was her. I tried to intervene when she was dealing with a Jack Russell. He'd found a vodka spill and was getting a bit too mouthy. I had to go to the vets."

Both dogs shuddered at the thoughts Thor's statement evoked.

From her lofty position in her human's arms, Millie snapped, "Then learn to keep your nose out, Thor! What makes you think I need the help of a Doberman with a god complex and a steroid habit?"

Rex said, "Wowza. That was a bit harsh."

Thor huffed out a hard breath and laid himself on the floorboards. Rex followed suit, demonstrating that he was calm and to be trusted.

The humans, who had been talking animatedly for the last thirty seconds all matched their dogs and relaxed, the tension in the room easing.

The man holding Millie, who turned out to be the landlord, placed her back on the floor with a demand to behave and went behind the bar to fetch biscuits for all three dogs.

Eight seconds later, the snacks consumed, though Millie was last to finish and eyeing the other two with a threatening scowl should either one attempt to snag a crumb from her pile, the dogs started talking again.

"So, Thor, before you came in," Millie started. "I was explaining to Rex about your theory with the people who came into the vineyard two nights ago."

"What theory?" asked Rex, seriously interested now. His human was good at figuring things out, but like all humans, he suffered from an olfactory inability. So far as Rex was concerned it defied logic that humans ever solved a crime - they couldn't smell the clues at all.

"Look I don't know the name of the place, but my human takes me there sometimes."

"Mine too," Millie chimed in. "It's got a long beach covered in pebbles with those big wooden things every few yards."

"Tide breakers?" hazarded Rex.

"That's them," Thor acknowledged. "Anyway, that beach has a really distinctive smell."

"It's the oysters," Millie chipped in her opinion again. "The sea there has a shallow bed where they grow. They are famous for it. The place always smells the same no matter what time of year it is."

"You mean Whitstable?" Rex asked. He knew of only one beach that stank like oysters all year round.

Millie and Thor looked at each other and had they been human they would have shrugged.

Thor said, "Maybe. I'm not sure what the humans call it. Anyway, that smell was all over the vineyard two days ago. My humans woke me up early. They were all flustered. So much so they forgot to give me breakfast."

Rex and Millie pulled appropriately horrified faces.

"They knew what had happened," guessed Rex.

"We raced to the vineyard and there were police there when we arrived. I'm not sure what makes them think our people would have stolen the wine and the vines, but as usual they were using their eyes and not their noses."

There then ensued a round of comments regarding humans and their stupidity. When it concluded, Rex summed up.

"Two humans you had never smelled on the premises before. A man and a woman. They had been to Whitstable in the hours before coming to the vineyard."

"That's about it," agreed Thor. "Except there had been other humans with them. I picked out half a dozen new human scents including the man and woman who came from Whitstable. They'd arrived with a large vehicle to take the wine away and another vehicle. If you needed me to guess, I would say the missing people went into a van. I was able to track their scents to a single point where all four abruptly stopped. Then I could smell where the van had been and there were tyre tracks."

Sitting at a table next to Rex – selecting it because Rex had chosen to lie calmly on the floor with the other dogs - Albert had enjoyed his pint of Kentish Ale. He wouldn't risk another, fearing the additional alcohol might tip him towards slumber.

His lunch had been served without Rex even noticing – a rarity - allowing Albert to polish off the plate of whitebait served with fresh bread and butter in absolute peace. The dogs, he noticed, were arranged in a conspiratorial huddle; imagining the dogs were plotting and planning amused Albert as he considered his next step.

Sticking with the theory that the Gastrothief would have his agents target a new wine connoisseur felt like a longshot, but it was all he had. If he was right, then it would happen soon, but who the target might be Albert could not guess. He knew such information would be researchable, but it was beyond him to do so.

He needed help.

Gary had done enough for him recently – coming to collect him from Blackpool was a jaunt to say the least, so when he chose to enlist some help, it was his daughter, Selina, he called.

"Hello, Dad. I was going to call you when I finished my shift. You beat me to it," said, Selina. She was still the apple of his eye, though her daughter, Apple-Blossom, the youngest of his grandchildren, was something to be cherished.

Albert wondered if there would be anymore grandchildren. His eldest kids, Gary and Selina, were too old for it now, and his youngest son, only just in his forties, was yet to find a girlfriend who stuck around long enough for it to get serious.

"Will I be seeing you, dear?" he asked. "I'm not going to be around for more than few days, I think."

Selina did nothing to hide her disappointment.

"Really, Dad? You've been gone for weeks. Where do you need to go next?"

Albert snorted a wry laugh. "That I don't know, dear. I shall have to see where the case leads me."

He heard her tutting. "The Gastrothief thing still. Gary did tell me there was new evidence. That's why you're back in Kent is it? Not to see your grandchildren."

She was being a little harsh, but he didn't want to pick a fight. He believed his tour of the British Isles was the first time he'd been away from his family in more than two decades, unless one counted an occasional summer holiday he and Petunia took when she was still alive.

Rather than argue, he said, "I think I'm nearly done, dear." He had no idea if he was or not, but it meant his response wasn't a lie. "The latest incident at a vineyard in Eccles might prove to be pivotal. It's one of the reasons I called, actually. That and because I would like to see you and the kids if you can squeeze in the time to visit the old man."

His tactic worked, Selina's demeanour softening instantly.

"Of course, Dad." She was no fool though and read the subtext easily. "You're about to ask me to help you get information or something, aren't you?"

Albert grinned to himself.

"Yup."

He explained about Simon Major and what he hoped she might be able to find out for him.

"I can come over later. I finish my shift in an hour. Shall I bring Apple-Blossom?"

"My goodness, yes, dear."

Selina promised to be at Albert's house – the house she grew up in – for around four o'clock. She needed to collect Apple-Blossom from her school and would do her best to find out about wine experts in the county. Hearing the gratitude and hope in her father's voice, Selena expressed that such things were not the usual subject matter for police enquiries – she might get lucky, but she was making no promises.

Thinking it was about time to get going – Albert wanted to get back to his house and perform some basic tasks such as laundry and sorting the pile of mail he'd found on his doormat the previous evening – Albert pushed back his chair and made ready to stand up.

A shadow fell over him, that of the landlord he discovered when he looked up. He was collecting Albert's empty plate and confirming all was satisfactory with his meal.

Albert thanked him and gave a due compliment – his lunch had been delightful. However, the landlord loitered a second longer than Albert expected.

"My apologies,' expressed the landlord. "I couldn't help over-hearing your question about local wine experts. It's a terrible thing that happened to Simon. He used to stop in here most weeks."

Agreeing with the publican's sentiment, but keen to hear what else he had to say, Albert pressed him, "You wouldn't happen to know who Simon's top rivals were, would you?"

The landlord made a thoughtful face, pursing his lips and skewing them to one side before answering.

"I'm not sure rivals would be the correct term, but certainly there are other wine connoisseurs known by reputation. You might want to check out Leon Harold. I believe I read he is being honoured with an award soon. That might already have happened, actually," the landlord qualified his remark, his eyes cast upward as he consulted his memory. "I can't be sure, but I do know that he works at First Press Winery in Rochester."

Albert wasn't familiar with the name of the firm, but he knew Rochester well enough.

"The other name you may wish to check is Camilla Humphries-Bowden. She is currently freelance, moving from label to label as new contracts arise, though I know a lot of companies want her. There is a lot of chatter about her palate being the finest in the country. She's twenty-two, so the world of wine is watching to see whether anyone is going to make her an offer she can't refuse. There are a few other names that I know, but those two are the ones I hear most often."

Albert got to his feet, signalling Rex to do likewise.

"Thank you, Sir," he pumped the landlord's hand. "I shall be sure to look up both those individuals. I will be telling people about this pub too. It's really rather nice here."

The landlord dipped his head, acknowledging the compliment.

"Take some cards if you like." He reached behind the bar to

snag a few business cards, handing them to Albert, who turned one over to read it.

"Timothy Gough." Albert looked back up. "Well done, Sir. You have a fine establishment."

There being nothing left to say, Albert gathered Rex and made his way back outside. It was at this point he remembered he was in the countryside and not only were there no taxis to be had, public transport was most likely something which occurred once every hour at most.

His realisation necessitated a return to the warmth of the pub, and a second, smaller drink, while he waited for a taxi to arrive.

4

AN OLD FRIEND

It was already dark out when the taxi dropped Albert in front of his house, the fare the same going back as it had been to get to Eccles this morning though the driver took a different route.

With a touch of dismay, Albert looked at his overgrown front lawn and the weeds growing through the small cracks in his drive-way. He could attend to them before he left again, but likely wouldn't find the time, or the required interest. It was all very well being houseproud, but he expected to be gone long enough that the pesky weeds would be back when he returned – why bother tackling them in the first place?

"Albert! Albert, old boy!" The call came from behind as Albert faced the house, but he didn't need to turn to see who it was.

Sliding his keys back into a pocket – Albert wasn't getting into the house for a few minutes he knew – he twisted around to face an old friend and neighbour.

"Roy! How the devil are you?"

Rex wagged his tail, recognising the man approaching as someone who was friendly.

The two old men shook hands, warmly greeting each other.

"I say you've been having a bit of an adventure, old boy,"

remarked Wing Commander Roy Hope. The retired airman had seen out the last of his service in the Falklands conflict in the early eighties, but still carried his rank like a well-deserved badge of honour. He stood five feet and ten inches tall, though Albert suspected he'd been taller in his youth, and had a full head of pure white hair. His face was dominated by a large moustache – also white, and there were thin red lines tracking across his cheeks and nose. Bedecked in tweed – Roy was rarely seen in anything else unless he chose to go with his blue blazer on which he wore his old unit's emblem – he looked to be a quintessential country gent. "Beverly and I have been watching with keen interest. We've got a collection of clippings from the newspapers, you know."

"Really?" It was surprising news to Albert who hadn't expected anyone in the village to even notice he had gone away.

"Goodness, yes, old boy. Mavis at the post office … well I'm sure you know how she likes to be in the thick of things."

Albert knew that Mavis was a diabolical gossip and it paid to stay on her good side.

"She's been telling everyone about my exploits, has she?"

Roy nodded. "Indeed, she has. "

Sensing that Roy was about to launch into a long-winded explanation, Albert got a word in quickly.

"Shall we continue this inside? I could really rather use the loo." The pint and half of real ale had worked their way through his body and were now demanding to continue their journey on the outside.

Safely in the warmth of his house, Albert listened to Roy prattling on as he dealt with a pressing issue and the Wing Commander scared up some tea.

"There should be some biscuits in the cupboard somewhere," commented Albert as he opened a door and started rooting around.

Rex heard the all-important word and wagged his tail, looking hopeful. Denied one of the sugary treats by his human, he feigned acceptance while noting which cupboard the packet was returned to.

After several minutes of bringing Roy up to speed, Albert admitted, "And that's what brought me back to Kent."

"Golly." Roy's eyebrows were hiked up high on his forehead. "A master criminal, eh? And only you out there to catch the blighter. I dare say you'll be needing a hand, old boy."

Just about to volunteer for the role, Roy's next words were dashed when the doorbell rang, and a voice called out.

"Grandad it's us!" a small voice called through the letterbox.

Rex barked and bounded through the house to greet the new arrivals. More people were always welcome.

Clapping his hands together gleefully, Albert started for the door.

"That's my Selina and her youngest."

"Oh, yes. Ah, Apple-something, isn't it?" Roy called after Albert's retreating back.

Moments later the house filled with noise as the trumpeting babble one can only get from an excited seven-year-old swept through it. Apple-Blossom had a million things to get off her chest and wasn't going to take a breath until grandad had heard and understood all about all of them.

"And then Chester said …" she stopped mid-sentence. "Who are you?" she wanted to know upon entering Albert's kitchen and finding Roy there. "You have a big moustache."

"Apple-Blossom," chided Selina. "That is not a polite way to introduce yourself. Try again, please."

Apple-Blossom dutifully recited her name and put out her hand. Once the task was complete, she said, "Why is your moustache so big?"

Selina rolled her eyes and mouthed, "Sorry."

Roy laughed at the young girl's precociousness – she reminded him of his own grandchildren and was about to provide what he hoped would be a funny anecdote about a crocodile. However, much like when the ladies' arrival cut him off a few minutes earlier, the same thing happened again, only this time it was Albert's phone ringing.

Peering at the screen as his phone vibrated on the kitchen counter, Albert remarked, "It's Gary."

Conversation paused when he answered it, Selina, Roy, and Apple-Blossom waiting politely and silently trying to guess what the call was about because Albert gasped more than once.

Albert, shocked by the news, while also guiltily pleased at the same time because he thought he knew what it meant, saw his audience, and begged Gary pause for a moment.

With one hand over the mouthpiece, Albert explained, "The Porker Sausage factory just burnt down. It's arson, but it also looks like a load of equipment was stolen and two people are missing. The fire brigade are searching the wreckage now, but I don't think they are going to find them."

Selina frowned. "Oh, come on, Dad. You can't instantly assume this is the work of your Gastrothief just because it's a place that makes food."

5

EARL BACON

E arl Bacon found himself to be in a changeable mood. When he learned of Simon Major's death it had greatly displeased him. He was quite vocal about his disappointment – the man was a pivotal element in his plan for sustainable wine production, yet the ham-fisted cretin Baldwin had allowed him to escape and now he was dead.

What use was the man if he was dead? Baldwin had failed to provide a worthwhile answer to that question.

After he'd finished ripping into Baldwin, Tanya had come on the phone. Earl Bacon liked Tanya; she had a can-do attitude and always said the thing he wanted to hear. Also, he got the impression she was utterly ruthless, and he applauded that in a person.

She assured him there were other candidates who would prove equal to the task of overseeing the earl's wine production and named almost a dozen. He eliminated all but two instantly for the simple fact that they didn't work in Kent. Kent was England's wine epicentre and that was where one found the best labels. The best labels charged the greatest price and that in turn allowed them to employ the best people. If they didn't work in Kent, they were clearly not up to the mark.

Tanya offered no argument, only a promise to make good on Baldwin's error.

Her assurances and history of delivering lightened the earl's mood, and his mid-afternoon snack was doing a good job of bringing a smile to his face. Moose cheese, the world's most expensive dairy product made by a single farm in Sweden, was complimenting his Iberico ham wonderfully. Drizzled with manuka honey and served on a bed of carefully hand-picked frisee lettuce leaves, it was enough to cheer up even the darkest soul in the earl's opinion.

His phone rang to cause an annoyed grimace. Didn't they know he was eating? It was four o'clock in the afternoon for goodness sake. What kind of Neanderthal didn't stop for a snack at four o'clock?

Grumpily sliding the phone towards himself with one pudgy digit, the earl saw Tanya's name displayed and accepted that he probably needed to answer it. Was it going to be another report of news he didn't want to hear? Or was she perhaps calling to let him know she had the wine expert in her care?

The latter was the one thing he considered might be worthy of interrupting his snack.

"Speak," he commanded rudely in his usual manner.

Tanya hadn't worked with many bosses who were as rude as the earl, but on the plus side he had never once made a pass at her which made him the first ever. He was heterosexual, so far as she could make out, but had no interest in sex because it wasn't food. The man lived to eat.

"The Porker factory is gone, and we have all that you wanted. It is already on its way back to you," she reported. "We took the current head of the family and his son. According to them," Tanya had visited earlier in the week to study the buildings, routes in and out, and confirm who it was that she needed to obtain, "they are the only ones who know the recipe. They made a silly joke about never flying together."

"Jolly good," murmured the earl, his thoughts already straying. His two favourite sausages would soon be available whenever he wanted them. Francis and Eugene had managed to successfully collect Jeremy Forrest from his house in Keswick weeks ago. He made the best Cumberland sausages and though in retrospect the earl believed they should have also taken his family – he would be more content with his future if they were with him, it was too late now.

The important thing was that the Cumberland sausage would be preserved when the world ended. Mad as a box of frogs, Earl Bacon believed Armageddon was nigh. He'd sunk his family's immense fortune into constructing an underground town. It housed those he 'saved' as he chose to think of the people his agents kidnapped, and was fitted with equipment to ensure they could survive below ground indefinitely.

There were still a few challenges to overcome, but the earl hadn't been back to the surface in over two years and had no intention of doing so. He was going to live out the rest of his days eating all that he could. His agents could risk their lives for him as they gathered the final items on his list. There wasn't much left now, all the big-ticket items were secure.

However, there were also a few things he hadn't been able to get. An old man and his dog had foiled his plans more than once, popping up unexpectedly to rescue a haul of Stilton cheese and then almost ruining his plans in Arbroath.

It made the earl cautious. Cautious enough to employ a new tactic at least. Now, when his agents obtained food or equipment or the people who knew how to produce the earl's favourite dishes, they destroyed the evidence. Where possible that is.

Setting fire to the Porker factory was an obvious move. He would have had them trash the vineyard, but Tanya assured him the work required to destroy the buildings and the fields was simply too great.

But the earl wasn't just cautious, he was spiteful too. When he first thought to start covering his tracks, it occurred to him that he rather liked the idea of no one else ever being able to enjoy the food that he possessed. He could not predict how much longer it would be until Armageddon struck, but until it did, he would be the only one eating Porker sausages.

It brought a smile to his face.

Snapping back to the present, he asked, "And what of my oysters?"

Tanya expected the question. "That is in hand. To be sure we get away cleanly, I am leaving the oysters until we have secured the wine expert. You have made your selection?"

"Yes. Please proceed as previously instructed." Earl Bacon knew which of the wine experts he wanted.

Tanya nodded to herself. "Very well. You still wish for us to destroy the oyster beds when we are done harvesting your crop?"

The earl popped the last piece of Iberico ham and moose cheese into his fat face with glee, making a fist with his free hand.

"Yes! Obliterate it! Blow up the entire coastline if you have to. Spend whatever you need on explosives. I want to see it on the news. My crop of oysters will be all that's left." He felt like laughing.

Tanya acknowledged her instructions and ended the call. The earl was the craziest person she had ever met. It was a good thing he paid well.

6

FISH AND CHIPS

Albert wasn't to be swayed by his daughter's doubts. He was heading to the seaside resort of Reculver where the Porker factory blaze was only just out. Gary had heard about it because he had his ear to the ground and a bunch of contacts dotted around the country. Friends and colleagues in other counties, though they knew not why, were good enough to inform him whenever there was any kind of crime involving the food industry.

"But, Dad, we just got here!" scowled Selina, unhappy that her father planned to leave before she'd even had the chance to take her coat off.

Albert agreed. "Yes. And thank goodness too. Now we can have a wonderful catch up on our way to Reculver. It's what … a fifty-minute drive?"

Selina blinked. "You want me to take you to Reculver?"

Albert walked sideways, talking to his daughter as he went to the door to get his coat.

"We need to be quick about it too. The Gastrothief's agents will have already left the area, but someone will have seen them. This is our biggest and best chance to crack the case so far."

"Wot ho," chipped in Roy, smacking his right fist into his left palm. "Let's get the blighters."

Apple-Blossom asked, "What's a blighter?"

Selina scowled at Roy. "It's not a very nice word, dear. Don't use it."

Rex knew something was happening and was in the hallway with Albert, spinning on the spot when he saw the old man get his coat and shuck his slippers.

Barking for attention, he asked, "We're going out again? Super. Is it somewhere fun?"

Selina checked her watch, sighing, "Dad, it's not the best time of the day to be hitting the motorways. I need to get Apple-Blossom home for her dinner too."

Albert zipped up his coat and grabbed his hat, pausing to answer with it held in both hands.

"We'll get fish and chips on the beach, love. There's that wonderful place in Whitstable." They all knew Whitstable was walking distance along the coastline from Reculver. A good walk perhaps, but walking distance, nevertheless.

Rex's ears twitched and he twisted his head to look at his human. "Whitstable?"

"It's too cold for chips on the beach, Dad." Selina could hear a whining tone creeping into her voice and didn't know why she was still fighting. There was nothing she needed to do this evening, and a trip with her dad sounded fun.

"Then we'll eat in the shop." Albert provided a solution with a smile. "They have seats in the back, and they let dogs in. Rex and I have dined there several times."

Apple-Blossom tugged at her mummy's coat.

"Can we get fish and chips, mummy?"

Selina's final argument would have been one about needing to get home to cook something for her husband and older kids, but she knew they would see her absence as an opportunity to order take out. They wouldn't miss her for the few hours she was going to be away.

With a huff of resignation, she let her shoulders slump and took out her car keys.

"I guess we are going to Reculver."

Apple-Blossom cheered. "Yay!"

Outside the house, Rex danced around excitedly. He loved riding in cars and the fact that they were going to Whitstable, the very place he needed to take his human, was a massive added bonus.

Upon his human's instruction, he ran to the garden wall and 'signed his name' before bouncing into the boot of Selina's family Volvo SUV. The large, modern car seated five with comfort which was a good thing because Roy announced his intention to come along before racing to his house.

He hadn't explained what he needed, but shouted that he wouldn't be long as he vanished through his front door.

True to his word, he emerged again less than ten seconds later, a flat cap on his head and a thin walking cane in his hand. He was talking to someone unseen as he backed away from the house, raising his voice so whoever it was could hear.

"An adventure, old girl, wot."

Roy's wife, Beverly, appeared at the door, a deep frown creasing her forehead.

"You're too old for adventures, you silly old fool. Get back in the house," she commanded.

Roy swished his cane through the air, nimbly wielding it like a young Errol Fynn fighting off imaginary attackers.

"I rather think you underestimate me, dear. I'm as spry as I used to be."

"You just want a taste of the drama Albert's been getting involved in," Beverly called out to her husband, knowing full well he'd been jealously yearning to join their neighbour on his travels.

Unfortunately, her comment played right into Roy's hands.

"That's the spirit, love. I'll be back in a few hours. Don't worry about the pot roast; I'll have it as leftovers tomorrow." He turned on his heels and ran to the car.

Beverly's frown deepened and she shook her head in disbelief.

"Have it tomorrow as leftovers? Just you get back here right this minute, Roy Hope."

Roy threw himself into the car, shouting, "Step on it," before his backside could make contact with the seat. "Under his breath, he mumbled, "Before the old bat gets hold of me and drags me from the car."

He waved gamely from his window and blew his wife a kiss as Selina, in the driver's seat on the other side of the car and oblivious to the exchange, pulled away.

Beverly Hope balled her fists onto her hips and narrowed her eyes. They had been married for close to sixty years and she loved her husband very dearly. That wasn't going to stop her from sticking him in the leg with a fork when he got home.

Muttering about the pot roast all the way back to the house, she went inside to plot revenge.

7

SLICK OPERATORS AND SAUSAGES

Rex slept in the car, the rhythmic sensation rocking him into slumber though he would have gone to sleep anyway. The humans were talking, his human doing most of it as he told them all about what he and Rex had seen and done over the last few weeks.

The topic turned to the case of the Gastrothief and that gave Albert the chance he needed to press Selina about the research he'd begged her to do.

"Oh, yes. There's a printed page in my handbag," she replied. "I had to call in a favour from a guy working in Revenue and Customs – he knows wine as well as anyone because he's the guy trying to catch the smugglers. Anyway, he gave me a few names and said they are the top people in the county. That's what you asked for, right?"

Selina's handbag was on the backseat by Apple-Blossom's feet. She passed it to Albert, who found the printed page.

There were five names, two of which he recognised – Leon Harold and Camilla Humphries-Bowden. The first was the man the landlord in Eccles said … *what did he say?* That Leon Harold was getting an award? If that was public knowledge, it might put him in the frame for the Gastrothief's agents to target.

The names had addresses and phone numbers, but Albert knew now was not the time to call them. He'd spent all too little time with his family in recent weeks and he missed them. His daughter and granddaughter were in the car, so he folded the list, slid it into an inside pocket of his jacket and made conversation.

Rex paid no attention. Like all dogs he lived in the here and now, putting no thought to what had gone before unless it became relevant.

When the car left the motorway, Rex's eyes snapped open. The change in speed and road surface meant they were coming close to their destination, but it was the smell that got his attention. He might have noticed it earlier if he'd been awake, but drawing nearer to the flashing lights of emergency vehicles, Rex's nose was working double time.

In the front of the car, Albert's nose was equally aware.

"Cor, can you smell that?" he asked the car's occupants.

Rex began to drool.

The stench of cooked sausages hung in the air so thickly a person could almost see the grease.

Apple-Blossom held her nose. "Mummy, grandad's dog is dribbling on me."

Albert twisted around to find Rex's head filling the middle of the rear screen. Up on all fours, the dog's nose jutted through between Roy and Apple-Blossom's heads, two horrible lines of saliva hanging from his jowls.

"Stop drooling, Rex," he instructed.

Rex's eyes twitched across to look at Albert, but there was a hopeless expression in them.

"I can't help it," Rex whined.

"Can't you make him sit, Dad?" asked Selina, worried the dog might shake his head and coat the car with horrible doggy slobber.

One strand of drool lost its fight with gravity, falling to splosh onto the leather seat two inches from Apple-Blossom's leg.

"Ewwww! Mummy make it stop!"

Roy's eyes flared. "I say." With a gentle hand on the dog's skull, he shoved Rex backward so the drool would at least now fall into the car's luggage compartment.

Rex was doing his best not to go nuts, but the heavenly, unctuous scent of fire roasted sausages had taken control of his frontal lobes and had shut off all his baser instincts. He needed sausages and he needed them right now.

The Porker Sausage Factory was easy to find because it sits on the main road into Reculver, a small seaside town modern life had passed by. Today, it was even easier to find because there were three fire trucks parked outside it along with half a dozen police squad cars. Police officers were positioned to keep the traffic moving as the emergency blocked half the street.

When she angled inward to park, a constable in uniform came directly to intercept Selina and would have turned her away had she not shown her ID.

Rex headbutted the boot lid, trying to make it open so he could get out.

"What has gotten into that dog?" Albert asked no one in particular.

Selina grabbed her door handle and paused before getting out. "Just wait here, okay? I'm going to find the person in charge and let him know I am on scene." Her rank dictated that she was likely to be the most senior officer present, but she had no intention of stepping on any toes.

Rex heard the driver's door open and felt the change in air pressure. On top of that, the scent of fire-roasted sausage quadrupled in its intensity the moment Selina gave the air outside a direct route into the car.

In a blur of fur and unable to stop himself even if he'd wanted to, Rex bounded over the back seats. Roy caught a swish of tail and a close-up view of Rex's rear end he'd rather have avoided. It was fleeting, the dog darting through the gap between the front seat and turning hard right to exit the car as Selina stood up.

With a whoosh and a shocked expletive from Albert, Rex was gone.

Albert hastily unfastened his seat belt, apologising as he fought to get out of the car. "Don't repeat what grandad said, Apple-Blossom, there's a good girl. Grandad said a very naughty word."

While the humans were hastily extracting themselves from the car, Rex could be best described as a furry missile. He had 'sausage lock' and was going in for the kill.

What he didn't know was how big of a problem the local dogs were already causing the police. The fire started in the early hours of the morning right around opening time and the building was an inferno moments later.

The dogs began appearing within ten minutes of the fire brigade being called as the roiling smoke carried the smell of ten thousand sausages into the air.

All across Reculver, dogs had abandoned their homes, forced their way out of their gardens, or slipped their leads during a morning walk as the smell filled their nostrils and whispered things to their brains they could just not resist.

Kept at bay by the steel fence running around the outside of the factory grounds, there had to be over two hundred dogs all salivating and baying to get inside. The police were attempting to coordinate with local radio to bring owners to the burning factory to collect their dogs.

On top of that, they had animal rescue on the scene, but the two teams that covered the sparsely populated area had given up when the almost rabid pack of hounds threatened to overrun them if they came too close.

Mercifully, they had corralled themselves into a spot on the far side of the factory. It was away from the road and where the factory's loading bay exited into the yard. The open door was letting the smoke and smell out and the dogs could all imagine they could see the juicy, half burned Porkers in the darkness within.

Rex ran directly for a pair of uniformed police officers who were manning a pedestrian gate. He couldn't know it yet, but the gate was the only way in or out of the factory grounds at that time.

When the dogs began to arrive, police and firefighters worked together to scare them out again and locked the vehicle gates which secured the perimeter.

"Whoa, pooch," said constable Bryant, closing the pedestrian gate before Rex could get to it. "GO on! Off you go home!" he gestured and raised his voice.

Given an order by a human – one in a police uniform at that, Rex had to obey. He looked around for another way in, and seeing the dogs assembled on the far side of the factory grounds, all looking longingly through the mesh fence, he went to join them.

Taking a long route to get around the police cordon, Rex nudged and squeezed to get to the front of the pack where he found a chocolate Labrador drooling hungrily through the fence.

"No way in?" he questioned, pushing against the steel fence with his skull to test its strength. There were a lot of dogs, maybe they could just combine their strength and push the fence down.

It held unwavering in its solidity.

"Not so far," whined the Labrador. "I want sausages!" His bark gripped the pack who were already driven half insane by the desire to fill their bellies.

The cacophony of barking that followed drowned out all other noise for over a minute. It petered out only when a Chihuahua squeezed through a tiny gap in the fence and made a run for the factory.

The dogs cheered him on.

"That's his fifth attempt," revealed the Labrador. "Every time he gets a little closer before the firefighters catch him."

The tiny Mexican dog made a break for it. Running with his head down, he streaked toward the building. The fire was out, but the firefighters were still working, checking over the wreckage that was the building – it was near skeletal in places. Everything was wet, the ground around the factory coated in a layer that was an inch deep or more where the ground was uneven. Inside the factory, water dripped from every surface and both the steel frame and bricks made noises as they cooled.

There were civilians unaccounted for which necessitated a thorough search of the structure now that it was safe. However, the whole task was being compounded by the darned dogs that kept finding a way in. The police were manning a pedestrian gate at the

44

front of the property – the only way in or out until the dogs could be dispersed – but they would have to open the main gates soon to get the fire trucks out.

Timing his run perfectly, the Chihuahua – who went by the name Peso - zipped between two firefighters and into the building. It was pitch black inside, but he didn't need to see to find his prize.

Shouts went up, the humans getting excited again. They'd caught him every time so far, but led by his nose, the Chihuahua found a split box of burnt bangers, grabbed a mouthful, and started running again.

The firefighters were partly concerned for the health of the dogs – there was glass and other sharp objects on the floor where the fire had caused lights to burst and windows to explode. But they also knew the fire had been started deliberately and the chief would have their hides if the arson evidence was damaged or ruined by an errant dog.

Seeing the firefighters move to intercept, Peso shifted gear and leaned into a hard turn. He was trailing a line of sausages like a cartoonist's drawing, and he wasn't slowing down for anything.

Chased by half a dozen lumbering bipeds, Peso shot toward the fence and perceived safety only to spot the hungry dogs on the other side all watching him and licking their lips. Only at that point did he realise the magnitude of his error. He couldn't leave the factory grounds – the other dogs would strip him of his prize instantly.

Banking into another turn, this one causing two humans to collide and then trip a third, Peso headed back to the factory and into the darkness where he found a soggy, but nevertheless reassuringly tight hole into which he could squeeze.

He could hear the humans calling for him, but his mouth full of sausagey goodness, he was going nowhere.

Rex watched the incident play out with barely contained enthusiasm. His mouth wouldn't stop watering. Pushing away from the fence, he announced, "I'm going to look for another way in." The dogs at the fence let him go, moving to fill the space he left as they remained transfixed by the smell coming from within.

In the street at the front of the factory, Selina was arguing with a uniformed officer of equal rank.

"I am not getting back into my car. My father's dog is here somewhere, and this is a public highway. I'm not even inside the cordon."

"Yet you are illegally parked on double yellow lines," pointed out Chief Inspector Quinn with a note of satisfaction. "Shall I have your car towed?"

Selina didn't know Ian Quinn, and working in London and not her home county of Kent, had never heard of him. She was, however, used to professional courtesy and officers from different regions working together. This idiot was doing everything he could to be pedantic and annoying.

Albert had taken Apple-Blossom with him and together with Roy, they were combing the crowd of onlookers to find Rex.

"Where has that daft dog gone?" Albert muttered to himself. The answer, he already knew from the barking he could hear, was the far side of the factory. He just needed to find a way to get around there as the police had shut off the street leading to it.

Making his way to the cordon, he spotted something and changed direction.

"Hello," he spoke to a pair of people wearing butcher's aprons and those white plastic hats you always used to see the local butchers wearing. Albert had spotted the 'Porkers' logo on their clothing by accident, but he'd badgered Selina into coming to Reculver so he could find out what had happened …

"Hello?" replied the female half of the pair. They were standing at the edge of the pavement, staring forlornly at their former place of work. Upon hearing his female colleague speak, the young man – her brother – turned his head to see who she was talking to.

Albert waved a hello and introduced himself, "I'm Albert Smith. I was hoping you might be able to answer a few questions about what happened here today."

"We lost our jobs. That's what happened," snapped the young man grumpily. "What's it to you anyway? Got nothing better to do than to come down here and watch people's livelihoods go up in smoke?"

Albert hadn't expected such an abrasive response, but before he could attempt to calm the young man down, the woman standing next to him gave him a whack. The backhanded slap landed on the meaty part of his left bicep.

"Oh, give over, Jimmy. It's not his fault the factory burned down. Go home if you're going to be moody."

Jimmy reacted with a startled expression and backed away in case there were any follow up blows to come. His arm was genuinely sore – his sister never did pull her punches.

"You've gone mad, Jen. Proper mad."

"Go home," she repeated, making shooing motions with both hands.

Jimmy flicked his eyes to look at the two old men now watching him, grimaced angrily at his sister and smartly about-faced. Without another word he started walking, rudely shoving his way through the crowd of people lining the pavement.

"Never mind him," remarked the young woman turning her attention back to Albert. "That's my brother, Jimmy. I'm Jenny. His girlfriend dumped him last week and he's been in a proper mood ever since. He's better off without her though. She had a face like a smacked backside."

Albert couldn't imagine what an appropriate response to her statement might be, so he reiterated his previous opener.

Jenny said, "Yes, you want to know what happened. Well, the building caught fire. We were just arriving and never even got into the factory, I'm afraid. The police are claiming it was arson. Me and Jimmy overheard them on the radio. They sent us home, but we were worried about Ralph and Evan, that's the owner and his son." She made a pained expression, obviously upset. "No one knows where they are and … are you a reporter or something?" Jenny asked, suddenly hoping she might get into the local paper and wishing she had done her hair and makeup first. Was it too late? Could she give a statement now and then have her picture taken later?

Disappointingly, the old man said, "No, sorry. I'm a ... a private investigator," he concluded after a second of wrestling with what the best term for his role might be.

"Really? Wow!" gasped Jenny. "You mean like Sherlock Holmes?"

Albert was going to play it down a little, he had nothing in common with the fictional sleuth's extraordinary powers of deduction, but Roy cut him off.

"More like Dick Barton, I'd say," he claimed with energetic gusto. "That would make me Jock Anderson, I guess, Dick's willing partner when it came to daring-deeds."

Jenny's face took on a confused look. "Dick who?"

Steering the conversation back on track, Albert said, "I believe this almost certainly was arson and it might be linked to some other crimes."

Jenny's jaw dropped. "Really?"

Albert knew that if he was right, then the two missing men were almost certainly still alive. He couldn't say that though – it would be too unfair to get the young woman's hopes up.

Instead, he said, "I believe so, yes. Are any of your co-workers here?"

Jenny, proving immeasurably helpful, led Albert, with Apple-Blossom and Roy in tow, to a café just a few yards away. There, gathered in a gaggle outside, were another twenty people wearing the same butcher's outfit. Most had coats on over the top to keep warm, and they were almost all holding hot drinks, but when Jenny introduced Albert, they stopped to listen.

"This is Dick Turpin ... no, that's not right, is it?" She turned to face Albert, a touch of crimson colouring her cheeks. Sorry, I've forgotten your name.

"I'm Albert Smith," he gave the assembly a wave.

"And I'm Apple-Blossom," said Apple-Blossom. "And my mummy is a detective chief inspector."

The gaggle's attention swung her way, their faces showing they were expecting more, but the young girl had run out of things to say and was now hugging into her grandad's leg for security.

Picking up where he left off, Albert said, "Did any of you see the two missing men this morning?"

"Albert is an investigator," Jenny explained. "He thinks this might be linked to other crimes."

A tall man lurking by the door of the café spoke first.

"Yeah, I saw them. They were there one minute, then they were gone. They weren't in the building when it went up, that's for sure. I told the police as much."

"Then where are they?" asked a woman in her fifties, her tone betraying that she didn't believe what the tall man had to say. "They've been missing all day and the factory burned to the ground. You need to accept that you missed them when you did your sweep."

"I did not!" raged the man, instantly angry. Albert guessed he'd been defending his statement from attack ever since he'd first made it. "When the alarm went off, I ran through the factory and checked in the toilets. There was no one in the building. That's how I noticed all the missing machinery."

"So you say," scoffed the woman.

Albert was content to stay quiet and listen to them argue - they were telling him plenty.

Barely keeping his temper under control, and probably curbing his language in deference to the little girl standing not two yards from him, the tall man spoke through clenched teeth.

"I'm telling you, Wendy, the factory had been robbed. The police are saying it's arson and I reckon they burned the place to get rid of any evidence."

Albert had no idea why they had set fire to the factory. It felt like a change in M.O. and he doubted it was because they were worried about getting caught. The Gastrothief's agents were like ghosts. There was barely any trace of the crimes, and he wouldn't have any more clue than the police had he not run into them in person.

Interrupting the fight threatening to break out, Albert asked, "Has there been anyone hanging around the factory recently? Have any of you seen … a pair of men probably." Albert was basing his guess on Francis and Eugene, the two men he met in Biggleswade.

They were his only reference for the type of person the Gastrothief employed. "They might have looked like ex-military?" he prompted, attempting to jog the collective memory.

The gaggle were looking at each other but no one was coming up with anything.

"Or they might have come into the factory posing as someone else?" Albert tried. "Has there been anyone asking questions?"

He was getting nowhere fast, but the last question had prompted a change in Wendy's face. She was no longer arguing with anyone who wanted to hope the two missing men were alive. Instead, her face had taken on the look of someone who was having an internal tussle.

Albert latched onto it, singling her out.

"Were you approached, Wendy?"

Wendy's eyes snapped up, a horrified look on her face as everyone turned inward to look her way.

"No," she snapped automatically, but Albert could see the conflict in her eyes.

"Was it recently?" he asked, his voice a soothing breath of supporting comfort – *trust me, I'm on your side*. "Did they approach you on your way to work? Tell me about them. What did they ask?"

Everyone else was quiet, waiting for Wendy to answer.

"Oh, this is silly," she remarked. "They were just a nice married couple in their thirties. They were interested in the factory and hoped there was a tour they could take. They said they'd been served the sausages at a restaurant the previous evening and had to buy some to take home with them."

Albert listened without commenting, but in his head he was thinking about how smoothly they had been able to extract information from an unsuspecting woman. They picked a lowly factory worker, not the head of the business who might ask why they had so many questions. They buttered her up with compliments about the product and marvelled at how many years she'd been working there. They took an interest in her. Then they asked about the factory routine and what time people arrived in the morning. They asked when the bosses came in and even got her to talk about the factory security system by asking about whether the place had ever been robbed.

They were slick and they were clever.

Albert almost admired them. Convinced he'd identified the Gastrothief's agents, he asked the big question.

"Can you describe them?" He already knew he was dealing with a couple this time, not a pair of men, but the description Wendy gave could match tens of thousands of man and woman combinations just in the county of Kent. The woman was attractive and slim, the man muscular. He was maybe six feet and three inches, she was five feet ten or thereabouts. The detail went on, but Albert knew it would do him no good. Without a photograph he had nothing.

Selina arrived, visibly shaking with rage following her conversation with Chief Inspector Ian Quinn and wishing someone nearby would commit a crime so she could smack them around a bit as she performed an arrest.

Apple-Blossom let go of her grandfather's leg to take mummy's hand.

Selina looked around at a sea of expectant faces before turning her gaze on Albert.

"What's going on?" she wanted to know. "Where's Rex?"

8

SAUSAGES!

Rex was less than fifty yards from Albert's location, not that he knew it or had even given it any thought. His entire consciousness was given completely to the task of finding a way to get to the sausages.

They were so tantalisingly close and yet seemingly impossible to reach.

He knew it wouldn't be sufficient to find a way in, he'd seen the firefighters chasing the Chihuahua. If he wanted to get to the sausages, he either needed a distraction or he had to get all the dogs into the factory at the same time.

It went against his nature to think like that – he didn't want to share. And that was when the solution came to him. There was a way in. He'd already gone up to it and been turned away. Looking across the courtyard at it now, he could see the gate was open again. Humans were going in and out in a constant stream. What they all needed was right there, but their nature, the thousands of years of living alongside man and keeping him from harm, dictated that they couldn't use it.

To do so would be disobedient in the face of the humans and fly against everything they knew to do as domesticated animals.

Nevertheless, there were sausages at stake. Rex ran back to the pack. It had grown by about another twenty dogs and was still being watched warily by half a dozen uniformed police officers as they waited for instructions on how to deal with the canine problem.

Barking in a frenzied manner, Rex ploughed into the pack.

"I've found a way in! I've found it! Quickly, everyone, follow me!"

The dogs didn't need to be told twice. Rex exploded back out of the pack, leading them around the fence line in a flat-out sprint. They had no idea where he was leading them, but they were going to get there in a hurry.

With faster dogs right on his shoulder demanding to know where the hole was and how it could be that no one else had found it, Rex continued to bark, whipping the pack into a crazed canine mass. It flowed like a multi-hued furry carpet, rounding a corner to burst onto the street at the front of the factory.

All the people still in the street had heard the dogs coming, one gentleman in particular unsurprised to find his German Shepherd at the front of the speeding procession. He even called his dog's name though the loudest bellow wasn't going to be heard by any of the dogs in the pack, let alone obeyed.

The cops keeping the people at bay and managing the traffic still flowing along the town's main thoroughfare, all paused to see what was causing all the noise and whether they were needed.

However, it was the two officers manning the pedestrian gate who needed to react, and they failed to spot the danger until it was just a fraction too late. Constable Bryant had remarked to his colleague in a witty manner about the dogs being 'barking mad'. It hadn't drawn so much as a smirk from his partner, who was at that point questioning whether he ought to shut the gate and throw the deadbolt to keep it that way.

Realising the dogs were heading straight for him as they sped along the street, he grabbed the gate and tried to close it.

The dogs at the head of the pack were three greyhounds. Right on their tails were a pair of Weimaraners and a Vizsla. Individually, the dogs didn't possess enough mass to prevent the gate shutting, but as the steel slammed against the lead greyhound's ribs and he yelped in pain, so a half dozen other dogs and then a dozen more besides hit the barrier with enough force to launch both cops off their feet.

Rex zipped through the portal a few yards behind the faster dogs. In the bedlam that was the race to get to the sausages first, smaller dogs were tripping larger dogs, dogs unable to corner as fast as the pack was moving found themselves buoyed along by the mass of dogs around them, and those who did fall scrambled speedily back to their feet, no concern for any injuries they might have incurred.

However, when an English Bull Mastiff stepped on a Jack Russell, they both went down. The larger dog's body created a moving hurdle too great for those behind to avoid with a resulting pile up of hounds more than a dozen deep.

No one snapped or barked or tried to lay blame though. Rex had been barking about their strength in numbers and how they would win by working together. As a pack they were stronger, so when the Jack Russell regained his feet, he didn't run off to find the feast. No, he bit hold of the Bull Mastiff's collar and attempted to tug him to safety.

Admittedly all he achieved was to dampen the enormous dog's collar and neck, but his efforts were duly noted.

Dog helped dog in the bid for flame-charred sausage and with firefighters and police officers running and diving to escape the seething mass of canine ferocity, the pack swept around the building and into the loading bay at the back where they fell upon the split packs of porky perfection like piranhas in a pond.

The whole episode was filmed by a local TV news crew who had been packing up for the day and were glad to be heading home.

Like everyone else, Albert watched in mute disbelief, catching sight of Rex only once or twice as the dogs ploughed onwards. Then he was gone again, rounding the building to get inside. With a huff of breath, Albert set off to collect him. At least he knew where he was now.

Sergeant Graves, a long-in-the-tooth cop nearing retirement looked to the animal control crews who were still hanging around idly doing nothing. They interpreted his silent question and had a simple response.

"They wanted the sausages. Let them eat their fill and they'll probably come quietly. It's not like they can be sold now they've been set on fire and doused with water."

No one could think of a counterproposal, so the dogs were left alone to eat. No one knew quite how many sausages there were in the loading bay, but when the dogs began to disperse ten minutes later, there were a lot of pieces of charred wrappers from the boxes they'd once been in. Little else remained.

Albert found Rex when the dog wandered out of the factory's ruined shadow with a full belly and a satisfied smile.

Rex wagged his tail. "Oh, hey, hello. Everything okay?" he tried weakly. "Um, there were sausages … and there were all these other dogs."

Albert glared down at Rex.

"You ran off, Rex. Do you remember you and I had a little talk about running off and how you were going to get lost one day? Do you not remember how long I spent looking for you in Blackpool?"

Rex hung his head. He didn't remember his human talking about the subject at all, but he was aware that he'd abandoned his duty to protect the old man during their most recent escapade.

Albert clipped the lead onto Rex's collar and began to lead him away. Rex hung back.

"I don't feel so good," he mumbled, the contents of his overfilled stomach beginning to rebel.

Albert interpreted Rex's panting for what it was. "Stuffed yourself, didn't you, you daft dog." Looking around there were other dogs lying on the concrete of the factory's yard. Dozens of them had eaten their fill and now wanted nothing other than to sleep it off.

Rex sucked in a few deep breaths, standing still for a few seconds until the wave of nausea passed. Tentatively lifting his head, he gave an experimental wag of his tail.

"I think I'm okay. Shall we go?"

There were police officers at the pedestrian gate beckoning for

Albert to take his dog and vacate the area. Other owners – those who had been unable to separate their dogs from the huge pack, were now coming to collect their pets too. The firefighters and cops would record it as one of the most bizarre incidents they'd ever attended, but all they wanted now was to get the dogs out of the way.

Albert led Rex back through the gate to where Selina was waiting by her car. Roy and Apple-Blossom were already loaded onto the backseat.

"We're leaving?" Albert questioned.

Selina opened the boot of her car. "Yes, Dad. The officers here want us to move on and I don't blame them. I think we've learned all there is to know anyway."

Albert's right eyebrow rose in interest. "You found out some more?"

Selina nodded her reply, however her focus was on the dog. Eyeing Rex sceptically, she asked, "Is he going to be sick?"

Albert gave a half shrug, but said, "It would be unusual."

Rex answered for himself. "That would be a terrible waste of food. Besides, I ate my fill unlike some other dogs who made complete pigs of themselves."

Had Albert or Selina understood the dog's strange chuffing noises they would have argued, for his gut bulged out on either side of his body.

When a cop waved his arms to get her attention and politely asked yet again for her to move her car, Selina accepted that she had little choice and let her dad put Rex in the car.

Rex sat with his head up to look around, decided that was uncomfortable and tried lying down. Maybe if he had a little snooze his belly would feel more settled when he woke up?

Selina reversed, turned the car around, and headed back out of Reculver.

Once they were away from the built-up area, Albert probed her for more information.

"Do you know Chief Inspector Quinn?" she asked by way of answering.

Albert shook his head. "I'm fairly sure his grandfather was serving at the same time as me, but all I remember of him are rumours about him being blindly ambitious."

The news did not shock Selina.

"I thought I didn't know him at all, and I guess I don't, but … do you recall that battle out in Cobham woods at the start of the year? There was a serial killer who'd been murdering women for decades."

"The Sandman?" Albert's brain sparked to supply the answer.

He got a nod from his daughter. "That's the one. The Sandman had a whole bunch of followers and some paranormal investigator got involved, I forget how or why, but there was a battle and the police showed up. Well, the task force that night was led by Chief Inspector Quinn. Do you remember what happened next?"

Albert racked his brains, casting his mind back, but no answer came.

Selina helped him out.

"There was a press conference afterward and something happened."

From the backseat, Roy gasped, "Is that where that fellow in combat clothes punched the police officer and knocked him out?"

Now Albert remembered, the scenes replayed on the TV appearing in his head.

"That's right. That was Quinn, was it?"

Selina flicked her indicator and joined the motorway.

"Mummy, I'm hungry," complained Apple-Blossom. "When are we stopping for chips?"

Giving the young girl a smile in the rear-view mirror, Selina said brightly, "Really soon, sweetie. We are heading to Whitstable now. It's about a five-minute drive." Coming back to the adults' conversation, she said, "That *was* Quinn. Everyone was talking about it at the time. The general feeling was that the paranormal guy, whatever his name is, needed the book thrown at him. Having met Quinn, I'm thinking I might have that wrong." There was a pause before she continued. "Anyway, he thinks the two missing men – they confirmed there were no bodies in the factory by the way. He thinks they absconded and set the fire to cover their tracks."

Albert screwed up his face. "It's their factory. It was their livelihood. What possible reason could they have for scuppering the whole thing?"

"Quinn suggested his investigation would find they were in enormous debt or being chased by criminal money lenders. And okay they wouldn't be the first ones to ever fake their deaths …"

Albert shook his head. "Not a chance. There were two of the Gastrothief's agents here."

Selina shot her eyes across the car to see her father's expression. "How do you know?"

"They quizzed one of the factory workers. She told them all about the security systems and when the place opened each day. They got everything they needed to know and then struck." Albert bared his teeth. "I am always one step behind."

"How much farther, mummy?"

From the back of the car came a sound not unlike a dog ejecting the contents of his stomach, for that was precisely what was happening.

Back on his paws, Rex had his head aimed at the mat in the boot as a torrent of barely chewed sausages made their break for freedom.

Apple-Blossom looked horrified. "Ewwww! Mummy! Grandad's dog was sick!"

Roy twisted in his seat to look. "Golly. That's a lot of sausages, old boy."

Albert closed his eyes and muttered uncharitable things inside his head.

9

FAMILIAR FACES

S omewhat later than anticipated, and after a trip to a petrol station with a jet wash to clean out the boot of her car, Selina parked near the seafront in Whitstable and left the car with the windows wide open.

This might be an unwise move in many of England's cities, but in a small seaside resort in late autumn, the carpark was all but empty and the likelihood of the car attracting unwanted interest was low.

Rex was feeling much better now that his stomach had returned to its usual size. He was even prepared to accept that he might have eaten one or possibly two too many of the succulent Porker sausages.

Bouncing down from the soggy boot to stand next to Albert, Rex lifted his nose and confirmed he was getting all the smells Thor the Doberman had described. The people who had come to the vineyard were here somewhere or they had been here in the hours before they left their scent for Thor to find.

"Where do you think you're going, Rex?" demanded Albert, tugging the dog lead to keep Rex in place when he started to move toward the beach.

Rex swung his head around. "I want to check out the seafront," he attempted to explain. "There was … look it's no good me telling you about what I can smell because even if you knew what I was saying, which you don't, you still wouldn't be able to figure out what it means."

Albert listened to the combination of huffing and whining coming from his dog and guessed wrong.

"I think he might need to look for an outhouse," he announced to Selina and Roy.

Rex tilted his head. "How did you manage to get that from what I just said?"

Selina's grumpy reply stole Albert's attention.

"Just make sure he goes, Dad. I don't want to have to clean anything else out of my car tonight and we still have the drive home yet." Arriving in Whitstable she had made the point about needing to keep Rex on his lead, almost sparking an argument because Albert always kept the lead on when he and Rex went outside. Rex would have been attached to his lead in Reculver had Albert been afforded the chance to do so.

A retort arrived in Albert's mouth, but never made it to his lips. His daughter's comments were unjustified, but he understood that she was upset about the rather funky odour filling her car. Perhaps a few moments apart would allow tempers to cool.

"I'll give him a good walk and meet you at the restaurant. Please order for me. I'll have plaice and chips with some mushy peas, please."

Rex seconded the motion, excited to sample the local fare. However, he wasn't going to get any; Albert knew that for certain. Rex's behaviour had earned him a brief fasting period. He would get kibble for breakfast and think himself lucky.

Man and dog set off, heading up and over the seawall and onto the path bordering the beach. Turning left, Albert scanned the darkness ahead and with a sigh of worried resignation, let Rex off his lead.

Rex bounded away down the pebbles toward the sea. The tide

was halfway out and retreating, a vast flat plain exposed all the way to the oyster beds.

Rex paddled through the shallow puddles, sniffing his way along the beach before heading back up the pebbles to rejoin Albert fifty yards farther down the path. It was impossible to be certain, but from the description he got from Thor and Millie, this had to be the right place.

The oyster beds were the big giveaway. The beach was littered with shells where restaurants and open-air eateries serving them year-round would routinely pile the shells onto the beach. They were taken away en mass each week.

Only now that he was here and feeling confident he'd arrived in the right location, Rex realised how little good it did him. Sure, he was in the right place, but so what? If the people who left their scent at the vineyard and were responsible for the thefts and kidnappings were here, how did he expect to find them?

He had no clue what they smelled like as individuals. Thor might, but Rex could see no way of getting him to Whitstable and who was to say the humans in question were still here?

Berating himself for getting excited over nothing, Rex rejoined Albert and stuck by his leg as they strolled along the sea path.

When it reached a natural end some half mile after they set off, Albert clipped Rex back onto his lead.

"Come on, boy. I need to get something to eat."

Rex wagged his tail.

"You do not," insisted Albert.

Rex's tail stopped wagging.

"You ate your body weight in sausages and then threw them all up in Selina's car."

Rex hung his head.

"You can have water," Albert concluded.

They took a different route back, winding through the back streets of the town to arrive at the main parade of shops. The smell of fish and chips filled the air, beating all other aromas into submission. It filled Rex's nostrils and made him hungry.

Approaching the shop with its small seating area tacked on the back, Albert wasn't paying much attention to anything other than his own rumbling belly and the desire to fill it with delicious pieces of flaky white fish and vinegar-soaked salty chips.

When a couple stepped out of the chip shop when he was ten yards from it, he barely registered them. Had they not frozen to the spot so suddenly, he might have walked right by them.

Instead, their startled reaction caused his eyes to focus and that's when his own surprise kicked in.

He started to lift his right arm to wave hello and his mouth was getting up to speed to greet the married pair when another part of his brain slapped those thoughts out of the way.

Tanya and Baldwin were relaxing after a successful day. She didn't want to eat her meals with the idiot oaf of a man, but their cover dictated they stay in role. There was nothing much on their minds except the final tasks on their list for Kent. They wanted to wrap things up in the next day and return to the earl's lair. Tanya hadn't told Baldwin, but she was going to demand he be reassigned to annoy someone else - she'd had enough. It was that or she was going to walk, and the earl could find someone to replace her.

However, the shock of seeing the old man they'd met in Arbroath yet again right where they were operating proved enough to startle them both into silence.

The old man smiled at them, lifting his hand as if he was going to greet them warmly. Could it be that he just didn't know and was here by pure coincidence?

Any hope that could be the case was dashed a half second later when they watched his expression change. Even if he didn't know before, he had just worked it out.

Tanya shoved into Baldwin, dropping out of character for the first time ever as she elbowed him to get moving with a shout.

"Move!"

Reacting on impulse, Albert reached down to unclip Rex's lead – the natural thing to do was to have his dog chase them down. In the instant after recognition, he knew for certain he was staring at the Gastrothief's agents. They matched Wendy's description and they were right here, just as they had been in Arbroath.

However, he lost Rex for days in Blackpool, fretting and barely sleeping the whole time they were apart. Then he lost him again today when the headstrong dog leapt from the car to find the sausages he could smell. And those two incidents were hardly the only ones in recent history.

Rex recognised the humans too – by their scent of course. Normally that would mean excitement on his part for humans he knew almost always made a fuss of him and often had treats. He would not have figured it out by himself this time, his doggy brain required a smell to connect the thoughts in his head. However, the way they reacted to seeing him and his human, and the old man instantly reaching to let him go triggered the connection anyway: these were the people who were at the vineyard.

His muscles bunched, getting ready to spring forward, but the command never came, and the old man's hand remained at his collar.

Albert's hesitation was all Tanya and Baldwin needed to make good their escape. Just a few yards from the chip shop, they turned hard left and barrelled into a narrow alleyway. Their accommodation, a small B&B overlooking the seafront was less than fifty yards away and they ran with terror powering their strides.

Tanya flew along the alleyway, making sure to be ahead of Baldwin so he would be the one to get bitten by the giant German Shepherd. Reaching the next road, she said a silent prayer and ran straight across it, trusting to luck that there would be no cars.

A glance revealed why she hadn't heard the dog's barks or a cry of pain from Baldwin – the dog was nowhere in sight.

Rex whimpered with excitement and struggled against the lead keeping him from giving chase.

"That's them! Isn't it? Shouldn't you be shouting 'Sic 'em, boy!' and letting me go? I can smell Porker sausages on them! They were at the factory today!"

Finding himself momentarily rooted to the spot by his indecision, Albert had soon recovered and given chase, but at the best pace he could manage - a fast walk. Jogging hurt his knees and hips, so he didn't do it unless it was absolutely necessary.

He got to the corner only a few seconds after the couple he pursued had shot down it. *What the devil were their names?* They were already nowhere to be seen, nothing but the faintly echoing sound of their footfalls fading into the distance acting as confirmation they had ever been there.

Rex continued to push with his legs, dragging Albert along until the old man gave the lead a good yank and commanded Rex to desist.

The couple had escaped, but that didn't worry Albert too much. They were right here in Whitstable, and he was going to find them. Besides, if they were anything like the two men he'd faced in Biggleswade, they were ruthless killers and Albert didn't want to try his luck without backup.

"Dad?" The sound of his daughter's voice turned Albert around. Rex twisted to see too. "Dad, what are you doing? Your dinner is getting cold."

Albert blurted, "I saw them, Selina. They are right here! It's the same couple from Arbroath!"

10
―――――――

THE HUNT BEGINS

Selina said nothing for a moment, processing her father's excited babbling though ultimately she came up blank.

"Who's here, Dad? What are you talking about?"

Seeing that he would waste too much time trying to explain when the ticking clock was very much against him, Albert clicked his tongue to get Rex moving and started back toward the chip shop.

Talking over his shoulder as he hurried back along the alley, Albert said, "I met a couple in Arbroath. They were staying in the same B&B as me. At the time I thought they were just a nice couple having a break from their jobs, but now they are here, right in the middle of two Gastrothief crimes and …" Albert shunted the door to the chip shop open with one shoulder, "they match the description Wendy from the Porker factory gave for the people who asked her all the questions."

Selina tried not to stomp too hard on her father's crazy ideas.

"That hardly makes for conclusive evidence, Dad. They could just be the same couple having another break somewhere else." She almost employed the word 'coincidence', but she knew all too well her father's thoughts on that particular word.

Albert paused his advance before they got to their table. Spinning to face Selina, he asked, "Then why did they run the moment they saw me?"

"They ran?" Selina hadn't expected that.

Albert nodded his head at Roy and snagged a chip from the untouched plate of plaice, chips, and peas.

"Like criminals before the law," Albert concluded, talking around the still-hot, greasy potato.

"Something afoot, old boy?" asked Roy, relieved he hadn't been shackled with child minding duty for very long.

Albert selected another chip, still on his feet and trying to decide what he needed to do in what order.

With a thoughtful nod, he remarked, "I've just bumped into the Gastrothief's agents. They are here and we now have a limited window to catch them."

Selina took out her phone. "I'll call Gary and Randall. We can't call on local police to help, not without explaining the whole Gastrothief thing and we still don't have any evidence."

It pained Albert to admit it, but Selina was right, and they were on their own. If someone like Chief Inspector Quinn heard they were using officers to hunt for the two people behind the arson at the Porker factor, he would want to be involved. They would have to explain who they were after and why and the whole thing would go south fast from there.

To be fair to Quinn, most senior officers would react in the same way and the predictability of the end result was so probable, he wasn't going to bother wasting his time finding out.

Stuffing another chip into his mouth, Albert took out his phone and thought about how it was that he could track down the couple.

If he had their names, he could start phoning hotels and B&Bs in the area – they had to be staying somewhere, but his memory refused to dredge that vital piece of information from whatever dark corner in which it had chosen to hide.

There would be a record though, he realised with a jolt of excitement. They had been at the B&B with him in Arbroath and he remembered signing an old-fashioned guest book when he arrived.

Selina was talking on her phone – to Gary, Albert thought as once again he racked his brain to remember the name of the place he stayed.

"Everything all right there, old chap?" Roy enquired. "You've taken on a rather pained expression."

Albert slumped into his chair, grabbing another chip to pop into his mouth.

"Mummy says people shouldn't eat with their fingers," said Apple-Blossom with a scowl.

Albert wiped a guilty, greasy finger on a napkin and picked up his fork.

"Quite right too, dear." To respond to Roy's observation, he said, "I'm trying to remember the name of a little B&B in Arbroath. The people here will have signed in there." He went on to explain his thinking and the chain of things that could happen if he could just remember the first thing on the list.

"Did you call them to make a reservation, Grandad?" asked Apple-Blossom, doing that world-wise thing kids do to demonstrate just how much they hear and take in when you don't think they are even listening.

Albert blinked his eyes, staring at his youngest grandchild in wonder when he said, "Well, yes."

"Then the number will be in the call log," Apple-Blossom explained.

Albert and Roy exchanged a glance. "My ..."

"Call log." The little girl held out her hand for Albert's phone, took it, and immediately started pressing buttons.

A frown formed on her forehead a few seconds later, prompting Albert to ask, "Um, what are you doing there, sweetie?"

Without looking up, Apple-Blossom explained, "I used your search engine to look up the prefix for Scottish area codes – Arbroath is in Scotland, right?"

"Last time I checked," mumbled Albert, baffled by the words coming from his granddaughter's mouth.

"Right, well then you either didn't make any calls to them or you wiped your phone afterward, Grandad. There are no Arbroath numbers in here."

Hazarding a guess, Albert asked, "Would it matter if I replaced my phone after I left Arbroath."

Apple-Blossom gawped at her grandfather. "Yes, Grandad. It can't remember a number it never dialled." Looking back at the phone cradled in her tiny hands, she started fiddling with the screen again. "Maybe I can cross reference via the cloud and ..."

Albert and Roy exchanged another look, both silently questioning if the other had any idea what the little girl was saying.

Their thoughts were interrupted when Apple-Blossom asked, "Does McClafferty's Bed and Breakfast ring any bells, Grandad?"

Albert almost thumped the table in triumph.

"Remarkable," gasped Roy, shaking his head at the surprising display of technology wielded by a child.

Albert's head flooded with memories. An image of the sturdy Georgian terraced house and Sarah, the landlady of the B&B. It was her boyfriend, Hamish, a local fish smoker, who was killed within hours of Albert's arrival. There had been no option other than to get involved, but just when Albert got to the bottom of what happened to Hamish, the man's son, Argyll, up and vanished.

They found his motorbike parked in the town centre, but of Argyll there was no sign. It had been troubling Albert ever since, but now he felt convinced the couple he'd just seen had snatched him.

It was the quest to uncover the Gastrothief that drove Albert to Arbroath in the first place.

"You have a stack of new numbers here, Grandad," Apple-Blossom remarked, a frown ruling her forehead as she stared at the phone's tiny screen. "They are in the cloud but not on your phone."

Albert said, "Um, they might be some of the people I met on my travels before I lost my phone."

With a silent nod, the child's fingers flew across the screen again.

"I've added the numbers to your contacts list and created a new group called travel friends where you can find them all more easily."

Bewildered, Albert mumbled, "Okay, sweetie."

"Do you want me to call the bed and breakfast place?" Apple-Blossom posed with her index finger poised over the screen.

"Um, yes?" Albert still couldn't get his head around how easily his seven-year-old granddaughter operated the complicated device.

Apple-Blossom held out the phone. "It's ringing, Grandad."

He took it from her just as it was answered.

"McClafferty's, good evening."

Albert recognised the voice instantly.

"Sarah, this is Albert Smith. You might remember me. I stayed …"

Sarah cut him short, "Goodness, Albert, of course I remember you. How could I ever forget? Are you calling to check if I've heard from Argyll, because I'm afraid it's bad news. There's still been no word. It's like he just vanished into thin air."

Albert was sad to hear that, but felt certain he would have heard were it not the case.

"Actually, Sarah, I'm calling about something else." Albert avoided details, he would get bogged down if he had to explain why he wanted their details, but Sarah dutifully agreed to look up who else was staying in the bed and breakfast at the same time as Albert."

"Suzie and Nathan Davis. Och they were a lovely couple, so they were." Albert knew he could change her opinion with just a few words, but he kept them to himself. Now that he had their names, he needed to use them to find where they were staying now.

11

DEAD AGENTS

L ess than three hundred yards away Suzie and Nathan were effectively dead.

"How on earth did he find us?" Baldwin demanded to know for the fifth time. Both he and Tanya were packing their bags, though packing was hardly the right adjective to employ. What they were more accurately doing was stuffing everything they had with them into whatever bags they could find.

This was an emergency 'bug out' situation – military slang they both knew for evacuating an area at speed. They were departing right now and would leave no trace that they had ever been there save for the B&B owner's memories and a credit card receipt under a fake name.

There had been a brief discussion about killing the B&B owners – it would remove the chance that they could pass on to the police any information about them, but the owner's car wasn't outside and the lights from their part of the house were out.

Tanya and Baldwin could not wait.

In a move that felt practiced, they checked the room, wiped down all the surfaces to remove their fingerprints and rushed back outside to their car.

Wasting no time, Baldwin powered the car out of its parking space, but once they were away from the bed and breakfast he slowed to drive at a sensible pace, merging with traffic heading out of the town.

"Wallet," demanded Tanya, prompting Baldwin to reach inside his jacket and hand it over.

They would ditch the car, parking it in a long-term place and walking away. It would be found weeks or months from now, but far too long after tonight for it to matter and were anyone to attempt to trace it back, they would find the same dead end and fake identification as anyone looking for them at the bed and breakfast.

From the bag between her feet, Tanya extracted a thick manilla envelope, upending it to tip the contents into her lap. New passports, new credit cards and driver's licenses, plus assorted other paraphernalia that went to create their new covers cascaded out.

Suzie and Nathan Davis no longer existed. Not that they ever had, but the IDs and cards they held for that couple would be destroyed shortly to ensure no one ever found them.

Tanya flicked her new passport open, gawped at it for a half second, and shot her head around to look at Baldwin.

"What the heck is this?" she demanded.

He flicked his eyes off the road for a moment to see what had her so excited.

"What?"

"This!" she raged. "The names on the passports and other documents, you utter cretin."

Baldwin let a snigger escape his lips. Truthfully, he'd forgotten that he'd had this set made up. To his mind, if you couldn't have a bit of fun playing make believe with fake names, then what was the point?

"You're Duke Ironhammer and I'm Lisa Delicious. Are you kidding me? We're supposed to be a married couple. Our names aren't even the same. How do you plan to explain that?"

Baldwin shot her a saucy grin.

"We both work in the adult film industry. These are our stage names, but we got so famous we chose to change them officially."

Tanya thought about just shooting him. She didn't have to kill him, maybe just shoot him up a little. There was one part of him she would quite gladly shoot off, but she'd seen his tiny appendage and wasn't sure she was that good of a shot.

Through gritted teeth, she asked, "And what happens when the pervy teenage son of the first person we show these IDs to chooses to look me up online? Our cover will be blown instantly, you idiot."

Baldwin double hitched his eyebrows with a grin.

"No, they won't, Lisa. I created a whole website for you and photoshopped your head onto a bunch of other models doing things … well, let's just say you are quite sexually adventurous in your new role."

Tanya wanted to ask if he was kidding, but she knew he wouldn't be. She would find the website and take it down as soon as they got back to the earl's lair. They were heading there now, their time in Kent unexpectedly cut short by the old man's sudden appearance.

She remembered his name: Albert Smith. He'd convinced her that he and his dog were just tourists bumbling around the country sampling the food, and she'd fallen for it. Questioning now if leaving the area was the right thing to do, she reached for her phone.

"I'm calling the earl," she announced, lifting her phone to her ear, and raising an index finger to silence Baldwin when he started to question why.

Baldwin had to listen as his partner, or Lisa, as he was already training himself to call her, told the fat member of the gentry what had happened. It wasn't a long call.

When she said, "I understand," and lowered the phone to her lap, Baldwin wasn't sure what she was going to say, but "Turn around," wasn't it.

"Turn around? As in go back to Whitstable?"

Tanya looked at him like he was an idiot.

"No, dummy. Not to Whitstable. Whitstable is far too hot right now. Go to Seasalter or Herne Bay. We'll set up there with these stupid ID's and carry on working."

Baldwin needed to check he understood what she was saying.

"The earl wants us to carry on despite Albert Smith showing up yet again?"

Tanya stared out of the windscreen.

"Not exactly. He wants us to capture Albert Smith and bring him back with us so the earl can interrogate him."

Baldwin thought that sounded easy.

"Oh, okay. That's better than the thing with the oysters then. Maybe he'll send someone else to do that now."

Tanya blew out a hard breath – a weary sigh of anticipated trouble to come.

"No, he expects us to do that too. He wants the oysters. He wants the wine expert, and he really, really wants Albert Smith."

12

BEDTIME

With Selina's phone set in the middle of the table and Gary's voice coming through the speaker, Selina, Albert, Roy, and even Apple-Blossom listened intently to what he had to say.

"Suzie and Nathan Davis appear to be fake names."

It came as no shock to Albert, but it was no less disappointing for the lack of surprise.

"There's no record of them," Gary explained, "But given time the forensic accountants should be able to trace the money backward to its source."

Roy was fed up being in the dark. "I don't follow," he complained.

Selina cut in. "They paid their bills in Arbroath under a false name using a credit card that matched it. Given the levels of security and protection in place these days, that's not something a person can achieve through a street corner criminal. Forensic accountants follow the money delving deep into where the money to pay the bill came from."

Gary continued, "There will be layers of sophistication to get through, but the money always goes somewhere. In the meantime, we can sweep all the hotels, hostels, and B&Bs in the area. If they were using the same name, we'll find where they were staying. Hopefully someone will know where they went, or they might have left a clue behind."

"We can circulate a description too," added Selina. "That way if they were using different names to the ones they had in Arbroath, we might still find them."

Albert wanted to stay in Whitstable and walk from B&B to B&B knocking on doors and asking if they knew the couple he was after. Intuition told him they were already in the wind – they would have cleared out the moment they knew they'd been made. They had been here though, and that meant he was right. He was right about the vineyard, and about the Porker factory. Better yet, it meant he was right about the wine expert.

Probably.

Albert didn't want to give himself too much credit. They could have been hanging around for something else, or maybe they didn't feel a rush to move on or were planning to go in the morning.

If that was the case, then he stood no chance of catching them in the act and it did him no good to think so negatively. If they had stayed in Kent because there was still a wine expert to kidnap, then he stood a vague chance of setting a trap for them.

Apple-Blossom yawned, the little girl's face splitting in two almost as her eyes closed and she showed the world her teeth.

"When are we going home, Mummy?"

Selina locked eyes with Albert. "I have to take her home, Dad. She has school in the morning, and I have another shift."

If he'd thought there was enough to gain by staying, Albert would have sent them away and found himself a room for the night. As it was, he saw the futility of staying in Whitstable. The couple – Suzie and Nathan – though he knew those names to be fake, would be long gone.

With a click of his tongue to wake Rex from his slumber, Albert accepted there was nothing left to achieve today. They would go home, and he would attend to some of his menial housework and laundry before heading to bed.

Tomorrow was a new day and perhaps by then he would have the name of the place the Gastrothief's agents had been staying.

Selina dropped Albert, Rex, and Roy in the street between their houses. Dad got a kiss on the cheek through the window, but Selina did not get out. She expressed she really needed to get Apple-Blossom home and into bed. Albert's granddaughter had fallen asleep just a couple of miles outside Whitstable, but they made it home without further incident and the car genuinely didn't smell as bad as they had all expected.

Roy tottered off to his house, thoroughly pleased with his outing, and acting as if he wasn't going to catch merry hell from his wife when he got in.

Albert, feeling weary now, walked Rex on a short circuit around the block before heading inside. There was no need to fix himself an evening meal – a cup of cocoa sufficed as he set his dirty linen to wash and settled with Rex in front of the television.

He was back home, and were it not for the Gastrothief case still hanging over his head, he would be able to claim that nothing had changed in the time he'd been away.

Settling into his bed that night, he possessed no idea of the bedlam that would come with the sunrise.

13

EARLY MORNING ATTACK

J ust when Albert was dropping off to sleep, Tanya was piecing together what she knew about him to find his address. They'd booked the first hotel room that an internet search revealed to have vacancies, and while Baldwin unpacked and checked their weapons, she settled in front of her laptop.

She knew his name which was a good place to start. His accent, which she first observed when they met in Arbroath, sounded local to the area they were now in. She thought it a little hopeful that he might live nearby – if he was staying in night-by-night accommodation just like them, he would be nigh on impossible to find.

She got lucky though, finding twelve A Smiths, each with an address. They were dotted across Kent, and the fact that six of them still had landline phones and were listed in the phonebook meant they were old to her way of thinking. She believed a landline phone to be an odd habit that would never occur to a person under forty.

Six addresses would take them a while to investigate, but Albert's dog would help. If they knocked on the door in the middle of the night and barking did not immediately ensue, she would assume it was the wrong house.

They employed the tactic, getting a bark at the very first house, but it was the wrong kind of dog – something small and yappy, Tanya surmised. They moved on and it was coming close to breakfast time when they finally arrived at the last address on her list.

It was a house in a quiet village called East Malling. Neither Tanya nor Baldwin had ever heard of the place and would have happily continued their lives in blissful ignorance. However, they were hoping this was the right place since it was the last one on the list. If not, and Albert Smith wasn't listed in the phone book, they would need to go back to the drawing board and devise a new strategy to find him.

"Stop here," Tanya requested, indicating a space at the kerb several houses short of their destination.

Ever willing to please, Baldwin coasted to a gentle stop and waited, watching the street ahead through his window.

The area was quiet, Tanya observed, and it was still dark out though the sky was lightening fast. There were lights on in many of the houses – people getting ready to go to work or send their kids off to school. The timing was suboptimal, but maybe they could get away with it.

No sooner had the thought crossed her mind than Tanya spotted the old man coming down the street toward them. He was out walking his dog, the hairy brute's tongue lolling to one side as he panted, his hot breath sending small clouds of visible vapour into the air.

Without speaking, she pointed through the windscreen, drawing Baldwin's eyes to their target.

"What do we do about the dog?" he asked, checking his pockets and sleeves for the weapons he had arrayed around his body and clothing.

"Probably kill it. I doubt the earl wants to interrogate it," she replied snarkily. "We wait until he is heading into the house, then we rush him. If we can time it right the dog will go inside, and we can knock the old man out and shut the dog behind the door. Albert will have his back to us and won't know we are even there until it is too late."

Baldwin saw no reason to argue, cocking his Glock 17 handgun and checking the safety before slipping it back into the holster under his left arm. He had no intention of using it, but equally had no intention of getting bitten. It was there if he needed it.

They watched the old man meander down the street and turn into his property through a waist-high garden gate.

Both Tanya and Baldwin gripped their door handles and were a heartbeat from getting out when they saw Albert freeze and turn around. He wasn't looking their way though, he was looking across the street, and they traced his eyes to find another old man, this one sporting an impressively large, white, and immaculately trimmed moustache.

The other man was waving a walking cane in the air as he hallooed from his side of the street. A car came along the road, keeping the two old men apart until it had passed.

"Morning, Albert," called Roy, up early and out because he didn't want to miss out on whatever adventure might be in store today.

Tanya gripped Baldwin's arm, keeping him in place as she wrestled with what course of action to take. She was all about making decisive decisions and seeing them through. Equally, she thought of herself as a clinically calm tactician.

She waited, watching to see what might happen.

"Any news on the case, old boy?" Roy asked, his interest quite genuine.

Albert flipped his eyebrows. "Actually, yes. I was just giving Rex a walk and I have a taxi coming shortly. My son found where they were staying. He called me not more than half an hour ago on his way to work. I'm heading to the station and then down to Whitstable again."

While the humans talked, Rex idly sniffed the air. He'd returned home to find the local cats had gravitated toward his garden while he was away. Rex always made a point of keeping them out, but with him gone, the infernal creatures had chosen to employ Albert's flower beds as their personal kitty litter tray.

They all got a jolly good barking at yesterday when Albert let him out, but they were around still – he could smell them. Testing the air, he caught something else too. Confused by it, he closed his eyes and concentrated.

The light breeze shifted, sending the illusive scent spiralling and he had to wait for the air to settle before he caught it again.

With a jolt, Rex's eyes snapped open, and he sprang from seated to standing. Aiming his nose down the street, Rex yanked Albert's arm as he strained against the lead.

"I say!" exclaimed Roy. "What the devil's got into him?"

Albert reached up with his free hand to massage his shoulder, questioning, not for the first time, if he just wasn't strong enough to have a dog the size of Rex.

Rex took a pace forward, dragging Albert sideways.

Over his shoulder, he whined, "They're here! Or they were here just a minute ago." Rex didn't know what it meant, but the couple he'd expected to chase yesterday when they ran away were here again now. He doubted it was a good sign.

Albert twisted his body around to face the direction Rex was trying to go and dug his feet in. "What is it, Rex?" he asked, his tone testy.

In the car, Baldwin was reaching for his gun.

"Let's just take him now and get it done," he remarked impatiently, toting the weapon in front of his face in a way that he hoped looked like a cool movie poster he'd seen recently. "I'll shoot the dog and the chap with the moustache. You grab Albert and we'll stuff him in the boot."

Tanya sucked on her teeth for just a second before shaking her head.

"No. There're too many people around. He hasn't seen us yet. Let's get out of here and …"

Rex's nose pinpointed the source of the smell and he lunged again. He hadn't timed it – he wasn't even looking, but he drove off with his back legs just when Albert was switching the lead from one hand to the other.

The leather handle snapped out from between Albert's fingers, freeing Rex who felt the tension vanish and assumed he was being given free rein to attack.

Tanya swore loudly and slapped Baldwin's leg. The engine was still running, but in the time it took him to get the car into gear, Rex had covered the few yards that had separated them and was leaping onto the bonnet.

He skidded across the near frictionless surface just as Baldwin shot backward in reverse.

Albert screamed, "Rex, no!" already mentally totalling up what it was going to cost him to repair whoever's car it was, but then he saw the driver's right hand and the gun still in it as he fought the steering wheel.

With a jarring crash, Baldwin smashed into Mrs Lovegood's Austin Allegro, shortening the front end by a foot.

Unable to keep his footing when the inertia suddenly changed again, Rex hit the windscreen, breaking the glass though it stayed in place.

With a squeal of rubber, Baldwin threw the car into first gear and powered away from the kerb.

Rex yelled in fright and lost his fight to stay on the car, sliding off to land awkwardly on his rump. Unperturbed, he leapt back to his feet and with his lead trailing behind in the air like a child with an unsuccessful kite, he took off down the road.

Albert, racing to intercept, came within a few inches of the car as it shot by. There was a moment of what felt like freezeframe when he locked eyes with the woman sitting in the passenger's seat. Then the car was gone, a spiral of exhaust and the offensive stench of burnt rubber left hanging in its wake.

Roy joined Albert, both men moving to block Rex's path as they shouted for him to stop and waved their arms.

Defeated by the car's speed, and under command to stop, Rex gave up the chase and coasted to a halt.

The crash had been heard by several neighbours including Mrs Lovegood who had been driving the same car since she bought it new in 1974. She tottered out of her house, still wearing an ankle-length flannel nightgown and slippers, took one look at her pride and joy, and fainted on the spot.

Sighing as he gathered Rex's lead and gave the dog a pat on his head, Albert said, "I think I might need to delay my taxi."

14

WINE CONNOISSEURS

The question Albert pondered in the time that immediately followed was whether he ought to tell his children he'd been targeted. He knew they would fuss and get excited.

To his neighbours as they gathered in the street to ask what had just occurred, he claimed to have no idea. It was a lie and he felt bad about that, but he could see nothing to gain by explaining his belief that two contract killers had been staking out his house.

That's what they were, he acknowledged to himself, and to Roy, who had witnessed what he thought was a confusing incident because he had no idea who the people in the car were.

Seeing the truth, Roy said, "So the blighters were coming after you?"

"That's about the size of it, yes," Albert agreed, patting Rex again as he questioned what might have occurred had his dog not been able to get the drop on them. "I'll need to move out again. It won't be safe here. It confirms my theory though."

Roy raised his eyebrows. "What theory it that, old boy?"

Albert rubbed his chin, trying to gather all his thoughts into one mental file.

"They still have business in the area," Albert summed up the totality of his thoughts. "They ran like startled rabbits last night when they saw me, but they are here doing the Gastrothief's bidding, and they are not finished yet. I believe they just added dealing with me to the list. Somehow the Gastrothief knows about me, and he sees me as a threat."

"Well, you have been causing him a bit of bother, old boy," Roy remarked, referring to the events in Stilton, Biggleswade, Arbroath, and more besides. "And you've been on the news on more than one occasion."

Albert grimaced and sucked some air between his teeth. It was true. He wasn't exactly a covert operator. His memory swung to Gloria, the former police undercover specialist he'd met in Dundee, and he smiled as he remembered how well she'd played him. That they had both come out of that adventure alive still beggared belief.

Forcing his thoughts back to the here and now, Albert said, "I cannot stay here, but that's no change from the last few weeks. I'm going inside to grab some breakfast and pack for the road. Then I'm heading to Whitstable. I need to check the place where they were staying and need to speak with the wine experts. One of them is in grave danger of being kidnapped."

"But which one?" asked Roy.

Rita Miles, the neighbour from the other half of the semi-detached house Mrs Lovegood lived in, went inside with her to make tea, and make sure she was all right. Albert said he saw the accident, but didn't know what had happened. It was another lie, but it wasn't as if Mrs Lovegood was ever going to be able to claim on the insurance of the other driver.

Her car could be repaired, so when the excitement died down and people with jobs to go to went back to their houses to get ready for work, Albert went back inside his house.

The taxi driver had turned up, complained about Albert saying he wasn't ready and almost caused a scene when he demanded to be paid anyway. Rex curled his lip and that proved to be sufficient deterrent, but Albert decided he would call a different firm next time.

Roy followed Albert into his house, offering to put the kettle on while Albert sorted out his things.

"Where will you stay?" Roy called up the stairs, continuing their conversation while Albert packed.

Albert didn't have an answer to that one. His focus was on getting to Whitstable because that was where he could pick up the trail. Whitstable was second on his list though – the wine experts came first.

Making his way back down the stairs, Albert said, "That I am yet to figure out. I think I'll just grab a room in Whitstable for now. I will need to be fairly mobile. It would help if I still had a car and still had the reactions to safely drive one."

Roy understood what Albert was saying.

Thanking Roy for the mug of tea, Albert placed his small suitcase on the kitchen tile next to his backpack and moved to the kitchen counter where he had a notepad and a pen. There were notes in it already.

He had five names, a combination of those he got from the landlord of the Red Bull in Eccles and those Selina provided from her research.

That one name cropped up on both lists he took as a good sign.

"We can phone them all … I'm going to phone them all," Albert stated," but my money is already on this fellow."

Roy donned his reading glasses to peer at Albert's notepad.

"Leon Harold, eh? You think he might be the one they will take?"

Albert huffed out a breath. "I think they are going to take someone. I have no real clue who, but I'm going to call a few people and see if anyone reports anything suspicious."

Albert studied his list, holding his phone poised in his hands as he thought about what he was going to say. He was a man trying to save a person, but the likelihood of coming off as a barmy old codger with a conspiracy theory was high enough to make him worry.

If he had a car, he would track each person down and approach them face to face. However, old father time had gotten the better of him, and whether he liked it or not, Albert was stuck with making phone calls.

Roy was watching with anticipation, but starting to frown as Albert continued to stare at his page of notes.

"Everything all right, old boy?"

Distracted by his friend's question, Albert was thankful to delay making the first call by a few moments.

He licked his lips in an absent-minded manner as he twisted his torso around to explain.

"There's an art to this, you know. The introduction of bad or worrying news is a tricky thing that can cause people to clam up. I need to put across that I have sensitive information and convince the recipient that I am both genuine and worthy of trust. Trust me on this – it's a tough balance to get right. The key is to be smooth in one's delivery."

Calling himself out for procrastinating, Albert punched in the first set of numbers and waited for the phone to connect.

A click preceded the voice of a bubbly young lady with a local accent filling his ear.

"First Press, where flavour found its home. Becky speaking."

Albert matched the cheerful timbre of her voice with his own.

"Hello, Becky. This is Albert Smith. I'm calling to speak with Leon Harold."

"Do you have an appointment, Sir?" Becky the receptionist questioned, politely.

"An appointment? For a phone call?"

"Mr Harold is a very busy man, Mr Smith." Becky's response was clearly intended to persuade Albert that his call wasn't considered to be as important as he thought it might be.

Albert bit his lip and went for broke.

"I rather think this might take priority over whatever else he might have planned for his day. I need to let Mr Harold know that he might be in danger."

There was silence from the other end, but only for a second.

"Are you threatening Mr Harold? I'm going to hang up and call the police. I have your number, you know." The line went dead with a resounding click that left Albert staring at his phone.

Roy lifted his mug of tea to his mouth, pausing it a few inches from his face to say, "Smooth, Albert. Very smooth."

Albert made a brief attempt at crushing his phone between his hands before accepting that not only did he not possess the strength, but that he also still needed it.

"More difficult than I anticipate on occasion," he admitted with an embarrassed smile.

The next call went better, the phone getting answered by the intended recipient and not a receptionist helped enormously. Albert explained who he was in abstract terms and was able to confirm the man he was speaking to hadn't experienced any troubling or worrying incidents in recent days. He didn't think he was being watched or followed, but understood what Albert was telling him about Simon Major and promised to be extra vigilant.

Feeling more confident, Albert moved to the third name on his list. Camilla Humphries-Bowden was another person named by the landlord of the Red Bull in Eccles, and when she answered the phone with a timid voice, Albert's Spidey senses were immediately alert.

"H-hello?" she sounded scared more than anything else.

Albert made sure to make his voice kindly.

"Hello. I do hope I've not caught you at an inconvenient time. My name is Albert Smith. Is everything all right? You sound a little troubled."

Reacting as if he had called her out, Camilla's demeanour changed instantly.

"No, no. Whyever would you think there was something wrong? You caught me by surprise is all. Is this about the BBC interview?"

Albert had her talking and that was a good start.

"No, Miss Humphries-Bowden, I am calling about a separate matter. Can I ask how well you knew Simon Major?"

"Oh, goodness. I didn't really know him at all except by reputation. A wonderful man by all accounts. The world of wine will miss him dearly. Such a terrible accident."

Whether it was a polished line she'd practiced in case anyone ever asked her about her rival or they were her genuine thoughts regarding the recently dead wine connoisseur, Albert could not tell. Whichever it was it had no impact on the reason for his call.

"Miss Humphries-Bowden I have no wish to cause you any alarm, however I need to inform you that I am investigating a connected case that leads me to believe Simon's death was not an accident."

"You mean …"

"He was murdered, Miss Humphries-Bowden. I can explain in greater depth when we meet," Albert pushed the concept directly into her brain without asking her opinion, "but the reasoning behind his likely murder leads me to be concerned that other leading wine experts in the region may be in danger. And that, of course, leads me to you."

Albert fell silent, intending to give the young women a few seconds to absorb the information before he pressed on. However, her next words were unexpected.

"Is that why I feel like I am being followed?" she cried. "Everyone is telling me that I am jumping at shadows, but I'm not!"

Roy saw the change in Albert's expression and came closer so he might also hear what was being said. Albert fumbled with his phone, trying to find the right button, and finally managing to switch on the speaker so Roy could hear Camilla too.

"You say you are being followed?" Albert sought to confirm.

Camilla was snivelling when she replied.

"I think so. No one believes me though. You said you are an investigator?"

Albert thought about how he wanted to play this out.

"Yes," he replied. "I'm not the police though. I'm more what one might call a private investigator."

"Like Hercule Poirot?" Camilla asked, trying to get the picture right in her own mind.

Unable to stop himself, Roy spoke up, "No, dear girl. More like Dick Barton!"

"Dick who? Who is that in the background? Who else is

listening in to our call, Mr Smith?"

Albert rolled his eyes and waved a hand to silence his overly enthusiastic neighbour.

"Sorry, Camilla, I have a friend with me. A side kick if you will."

Rex frowned deeply from his comfortable position stretched out on the cool kitchen tile. If Roy was the sidekick, what did that make him? So far as Rex was concerned, Albert was the sidekick and Rex was the detective. Roy was a comedy distraction at best.

The humans were paying him no attention, so he put his head back down and closed his eyes.

"I have no wish to alarm you, but I have good reason to believe Simon Major's death was not accidental and occurred because someone wanted to kidnap him."

Camilla drew in a sudden and shocked lungful of air. "Oh, my goodness. Why would someone want to do that?"

Albert switched tack. "I think it imperative that I meet with you, Miss Humphries-Bowden. Is there somewhere you would feel safe?"

She fell silent for a few seconds to consider the question.

"I guess where I am now is where I feel safest. I am home," she added quickly, realising she had left out that vital piece of information.

"And you say you believe you are being followed?" Albert wanted her to tell him as much as possible.

With a trembling voice, Camilla Humphries-Bowden, a rising star in the world of wine, told Albert all about the intangible sense of dread she'd recently developed. There was someone following her, she knew it for certain, but she hadn't seen them and couldn't guess who it might be.

She made it sound like there was someone just out of sight – there, but never overtly. She'd told her parents and her brother and even contacted the police, but by her own admission she didn't have anything to tell them. Just a sense of dread.

Albert asked her to stay where she was, told her to look out for two older gentlemen with a dog and ended the call. He had her address just outside Sandwich and would get there just as soon as he could.

"You think she's the one then?" Roy asked when Albert put his phone down. "Not that other fellow?"

Albert's gut told him she was, but he knew to not let emotion rule his head. Years of police work had shown him how often the clues could lead to the wrong conclusion.

What he said was, "We need to check the others." In the next five minutes, he made contact with the remaining two persons on his list. Neither of them sounded like they were candidates for kidnap. The fourth name on the list turned out to be a man in his eighties who had recently retired, and the final name was on holiday in Scotland visiting family.

It left Albert with the probable-looking Camilla, and the completely unknown Leon.

"What do we do about him then, old boy?"

Albert started putting his things into his pockets and made sure the back door was locked.

"Nothing. That's why we go to him first. It's not far to Rochester and we can get the train from there instead. It's a direct route to Whitstable that way. I'll find a B&B and it's a short hop to Sandwich then. Camilla said she wouldn't leave the house, so I think she'll be safe until we get there."

"What do we do about her if you think she is the one they are after? Can one of your children arrange a safe house?"

Albert picked up his suitcase and backpack. "There's no justification to even apply for one. The Gastrothief case is still off the books. At best they might be able to arrange for someone to put a plain clothes officer to watch her for a few days."

Leaving the house a few moments later with a plan to walk to East Malling train station half a mile away because they would almost certainly find a taxi waiting, they were surprised to find their path blocked.

As their feet ground to a halt, Albert and Roy snuck a glance at each other. No words needed to be spoken – it was clear from the angry glare and surly expression aimed their way that both men were in trouble.

15

LEON HAROLD

"Where do you two reprobates think you are going?" demanded Beverly Hope, her arms folded tightly across her chest.

Roy leaned his head toward Albert. "Just watch the arms, old boy," he whispered. "We'll be all right if she keeps them crossed."

Beverly chose that moment, spurred on by seeing her husband whispering something, to unfold her arms and ready her wagging finger.

"Oh, cripes," Roy gulped. "Look out, old boy. Every man for himself."

"Don't you move from that spot Wing Commander Hope!" warned Beverly, wagging her right index finger at him.

Roy had been about to conduct a hasty exit-stage-right to go around the back of Albert's house and over the garden fence - his plan to emerge farther down the street. Caught before he could get moving, he lowered his right foot to the ground once more.

With a smile, he tried, "Hello, my apple dumpling. Is everything all right?"

He got wagged at again. "Don't you try to sweet talk me, Roy Hope. The days when your cheeky smile could win me over ended five decades ago. Where is it that you think you are going? I can see Albert's suitcase in his hand. You were out galivanting yesterday evening. That's quite enough adventure for one week."

"But there are criminals to catch, darling," Roy protested.

"And since when was that your job?" Beverly demanded.

Roy directed her attention to Albert, saying, "You've read the newspaper articles, darling. You know what he's been up against. A chap can't let his good friend face the enemy alone, old girl."

Beverly shook her head. "Galivanting. That's all it is. Two daft old men getting into trouble because they've had one too many sherries with their lunch. Get back in the house, Roy Hope, I've got housework for you."

Albert spoke out of the side of his mouth.

"Perhaps I should head to Whitstable by myself, Roy."

Roy was attempting to fashion an argument that would work when his wife cut him off.

"Whitstable? Did you say you are going to Whitstable?" Her question was aimed squarely at Albert, her left hand up and palm out to warn Roy that staying quiet would be a good policy to employ.

Albert risked a glance at his partner in crime – though he wasn't entirely sure what crime they had been committing.

"Um, yes. Among other places …" Albert's voice trailed off as Roy's wife spun on her toes to head back to her house.

"I'll drive then. Roy's been promising to take me to the fish market there for months. We'll have a nice piece of skate wing for dinner."

Both men were lost for words at the unexpected turn of events. Thrown off balance, Albert frowned at Roy.

"I guess we don't need the taxi or the train then. Will she take us where we need to go, or do you think this will turn into a shopping trip?"

Roy shrugged, lifting his shoulders until they came level with his ears.

"Your guess is as good as mine, old boy. Best to play along

though. If we sneak off now, I'll be eating cabbage soup for a month."

Albert curled his lip. "Cabbage soup?"

Roy nodded his head with a rueful expression. "Yes. Beverly knows how to hurt me. Push her too far and the kitchen goes on strike."

The door to the Hope residence opened again and Beverly bustled out wearing a coat and matching hat. She had a handbag hooked over her left arm and a set of car keys in her right hand.

The lights on their 2006 Mercedes E Class flashed twice and she hit the men with a meaningful stare.

"Well get in then, you pair of ninnies."

Arriving at First Press Wines on the outskirts of Rochester just twelve minutes after setting off, Albert had to concede that having Beverly as a chauffeur beat walking to find a taxi and then getting a train or any combination of other travel options. Roy's wife wanted to visit the fish market in the harbour, but it became quickly clear that she also wanted to get out of the house and have something different to do.

In the short first leg of their trip, Beverly quizzed Albert on his tour around the British Isles, focussing largely on the places and the food rather than the murders and investigations. She spoke about travelling in a wistful manner, commenting that she and Roy used to pack their bags regularly, but hadn't been anywhere in years.

She was quite clear that she considered it to be Roy's fault though she held back from directly saying so. Roy remained uncharacteristically quiet.

Unlike the vineyard in Eccles which had the appearance of a working farm, the premises of First Press Wines was dominated by a large, glass-fronted office building. People in office-wear could be seen going back and forth inside, and there was a young woman sitting behind a marble desk.

Pushing through the glass front door, Albert kept Rex on a short lead, instructing that he needed to "behave" while they were in the building.

Rex had no idea what the old man could be suggesting and was too busy sniffing the air to reply. There were no other animals here, nor had there been for some time. He could smell the wine fermenting a quarter mile distant, and the vinyl smell of freshly unboxed marketing material stacked in a conference room to his left. The young woman sitting at the reception desk had a half-eaten chocolate bar hidden in her drawer and he could detect and separate more than a dozen humans just from their individual scents – a combination of cologne, other scented products, and their natural body odour.

Rex performed the scent check in the first few seconds while they were still walking across the marble floor of the building's lobby.

"Coo, this place is plush," remarked Beverly. "No wonder their wines are so expensive."

The young woman smiling politely from behind reception had 'Becky' on her name badge. Albert figured she had to be the same woman he had spoken to on the phone and addressed her as such.

"Hello, I'm Albert Smith. We spoke on the phone just a short while ago and we managed to get our wires crossed."

A moment of confusion filled Becky's eyes as she attempted to decipher what the old man was saying. Then her brain lined up the pertinent clues and her right hand shot out to grab her phone.

"You're the one who threatened Leon! I can call security!" she warned.

Albert raised both his hands. "I'm nearly eighty, Becky. I wasn't threatening anyone. I need to speak with Mr Harold because he may be in danger, just not from me. I wouldn't be here in person if it were not of paramount importance."

Her hand kept hold of the phone, but Albert could see she was adding the visual clues to what she thought she knew and was heading toward the right decision.

"I only need a few moments of his time," he added, tipping her over the edge.

"Okay," she relented. "I'll need to see if he is free."

Albert, Roy, Beverly, and Rex retired to a set of chairs a few yards away where visitors were invited to help themselves to refreshments and entertain their eyes by looking through the tempting pictures in the marketing brochures.

Killing time, Albert picked up a magazine entitled 'Wine and Country'. It was not a publication he was familiar with, suspecting it to be an industry thing that no one on the outside would find interesting. Intending to leaf through it, Albert got as far as looking at the front page when a man entered reception.

"You said there is someone to see me, Becky?" he asked loudly enough for Albert to hear.

The man was in his fifties and wearing an elegant royal blue suit. Directed toward the visitors' area by a nod of Becky's head, he adjusted his trajectory. Seeing the man's face properly, Albert performed a double take and lifted the magazine he held in his right hand.

The man smiling out from the cover was the same one now walking toward him. It even had his name in bold letters though Albert hadn't thought to read it.

"Ah," Leon Harold boomed, gleefully. "I see you are fans." He was referring to the magazine Albert held. "Hello," he greeted the visitors warmly, unsure what they wanted from Becky's garbled message, but willing to give them the benefit of the doubt. "I believe one of you has a message for me?"

Albert had placed the magazine back on the low table and was already getting to his feet, allowing Rex's forward motion to assist his rise. Extending his right arm, he shook hands with the wine expert.

The wine connoisseur clearly expected gushing praise or fanboy adulation. Albert chose to get straight to the matter at hand.

"Mr Harold I'm sure you are aware of Simon Major's tragic accident."

Leon Harold dropped his smile, replacing it with a suitable sombre expression.

"Goodness, yes. It's simply terrible. I heard there was a robbery though. Are the police sure it was an accident."

Nicely cued up, Albert got straight to the point. "You are an astute man, Mr Harold, so I'll waste no time beating around the bush. I have reason to believe that Simon Major died during an attempted kidnapping. I am a retired senior police detective now working for a … private client." It wasn't a lie exactly. That Albert was his own client did not need to be announced. "I've no wish to alarm you, Sir, but I must ask whether you have been witness to anyone watching you or following you? Whether you have noticed anything out of the ordinary or have had anyone asking questions about your routine in the recent days or weeks?"

Leon Harold's face had taken on a slightly stunned look, his facial muscles unsure which emotion they ought to be portraying.

"Attempted kidnapping? Why would someone want to kidnap Simon Major? He doesn't have a rich family who might pay a ransom. Does he?" Leon added a question at the end as if unsure of his own beliefs.

Albert said, "I cannot comment on Simon's family fortune or otherwise, but ransom would not have been the intention." Before Leon could pose his next question, Albert did his best to explain in loose terms. "I have been tracking a gang," he chose the word 'gang' for its all-encompassing nature, "across the British Isles and beyond. For purposes I am yet to determine, they have been taking food, equipment, and people from various businesses." Albert then rattled off half a dozen different incidents that he had been able to uncover. "Many of them could be dismissed as coincidence, but when viewed as a whole …"

Leon Harold appeared to be gobsmacked, but one question made it through the fog of his confusion.

"You think they might target me?"

Albert nodded his head. "I fear that may be the case, yes. I believe they were after Simon Major, but having failed to take him alive, they might now default to you."

Leon stared into space for a few more seconds, but then his expression changed.

"Wait a minute," he said, his brow furrowing. "This is some kind of scam, isn't it? If I was really in any danger the police would be here, not some pensioners."

Albert sucked some air between his teeth. "I am not attempting to extract money from you, Mr Harold. Nor do I wish for you to do anything other than to be mindful of your surroundings and to share with me that information I first requested – whether you have seen or heard anything that might fit with what I have just told you?"

A smile spread across Leon's face, and he started to wag a finger knowingly.

"You almost had me there. Who put you up to this? Is it the same bunch who wanted to convince everyone Simon was the number one wine connoisseur? If he was soooo good, why am I the one getting the award this afternoon, huh? Why is my face on the cover of Wine and Country and not his?"

Flustered by the change of direction, Albert said, "Sir, I can assure you …" but Leon Harold had already stopped listening.

Not only that, the wine expert was walking away, going backwards as he delivered his parting comments.

"Putting me off my game right before the awards ceremony event tonight? That's a dirty trick, you know. Go back to whoever sent you and tell them they'll need to try a lot harder if they want to catch Leon Harold out."

"Mr Harold," Albert called after the man as he spun to face the other way and walked off without looking back. "Mr Harold this is a serious matter." Albert's words fell on deaf ears and the wine expert left the reception area through a door on the right, escaping from sight with no intention of listening to anything anyone had to say.

Albert cursed under his breath.

Coming to stand next to him, Roy said, "That chap's a bit of a plonker, wouldn't you say?"

Albert pursed his lips and racked his brains. Did it matter? Was Leon Harold ever the target? Camilla Humphries-Bowden was being stalked – almost certainly by the Gastrothief's agents, so if he focused on her instead, it might be the best use of his time.

With a click of his tongue to get Rex moving, Albert said, "I think we should press on. The day is short, and I have lots of ground to cover."

16

A BIG CLUE?

D riving as if she worried the fish market might close before she got there, Beverly's heavy right foot got them to Whitstable before noon. Making their way to the seafront, they passed the bed and breakfast Albert was to visit. He noted where it was – expecting to have to find it again shortly, but wouldn't need a map because Beverly pulled into a carpark less than fifty yards later.

"I always park here," she announced, aiming the large German car at a vacant spot. "It's right next to the Oyster House. We can have a nice lunch since we are here. Can't we, Roy?" she added, dropping her voice an octave so her polite question came out as a command instead.

Albert grabbed his door handle. "I'll leave my bags here, if that's all right?"

Roy twisted around to look at his friend on the back seat. Not that he could see Albert. Rex was on his feet, excited to get out and standing over his human while he waited for someone to open the door.

"I thought you were planning to stay at the same B&B the Gastrothief's agents just left?" Roy asked, levering himself up to look over Rex's back.

Albert gave Rex a shove so he could exit first and not have his wotsits crushed when Rex trampled over him to get out.

"That was my plan, but they said they are full when I called this morning. Apparently, there's some event on this weekend and all the places are filling up fast."

"It's the Whitstable Autumn Festival," remarked Beverly in a tone that suggested they ought to know. "Have you not noticed the posters?"

Clambering out with Rex shunting and shoving to get past, Albert stood up and looked around. In the darkness last night, he hadn't noticed, but there were indeed posters displaying the date and the festival in lurid colours. Not only that, there was bunting adorning a dozen buildings in the immediate vicinity.

"To the B&B first then, old boy?" Roy confirmed the plan.

Albert shot his eyes at Beverly, certain Roy's plan failed to match hers.

"Luncheon, Wing Commander Hope," she stated firmly. Then with a softer tone asked, "Will you join us, Albert?"

Albert shook his head, certain that he would be intruding. More than that, he just wasn't prepared to delay his investigation any longer.

"Thank you, Beverly, but no, I must decline. I had rather a large breakfast," he added to make his response seem more justified.

Roy was a little put out. "So, we'll um … we'll see you afterward?" The need to push on to Sandwich, another resort just a few miles down the coast had been discussed in the car.

"Indeed?" replied Albert, his eyes trained on Beverly so she could confirm that was still the plan.

"Once we've had lunch and visited the fish market," she replied.

With the batting order set, Roy and Beverly went in one direction, Albert and Rex in the other.

Rex's nose was working hard, sniffing, sifting, and recording the numerous smells assailing his nostrils.

The tide was in which meant the mud flats and oyster beds were covered, the scent from them reduced to nothing though Rex could still detect the smell where people had walked out to the beds and then back up the beach, trailing the mud with them. All around was the smell of dogs, fish, food, oyster, and the salty tang of the sea.

Leading where his human instructed, Rex left the beach via a set of stone steps, climbing to an apex to crest the sea wall and then down the other side where the onshore breeze dropped significantly.

He recognised where they were. Whitstable obviously, but more specifically than that. They were back near the alley where he wanted to chase the couple who ran from him last night. Rex wasn't sure what that was about, but they had been outside his house today and that elevated their threat status.

If they meant his human harm, they were going to have to go through him first.

Rex's nose led him to the bed and breakfast place where Tanya and Baldwin had been staying, Albert followed along behind without noticing the dog had taken him exactly where he wanted to go.

The sign on the front façade of the building – a large Georgian terraced house set over four floors – confirmed they were in the right place and the door was answered a few moments after Albert rang the bell.

"Mr Smith, is it?" asked the lady now filling the doorway. The house was set in such a way that the first floor was raised more than a yard from the height of the street in case of flood tides. Albert had climbed the steps to press the bell and descended halfway again so he wasn't in the owner's face when she opened the door.

He knew the lady to be Alice Scott. She ran the B&B with her husband Glen, but she was considerably older than Albert had imagined and had to be in her seventies. Dressed in a pair of light brown slacks with a crease down the front of each leg and a knitted jumper over a roll-neck top – both in cream hues – Alice was casual but elegant. A simple pearl necklace and pearl studs that had the look of heirlooms passed down by a previous generation completed the picture.

Albert came up the steps, extending his hand.

"Yes. I'm Albert. Pleased to meet you. Thank you so much for agreeing to let me see the room."

Alice backed away from the door, holding it open so Albert could come inside.

"I was beginning to worry the guests would get here before you. I advertised the room as vacant last night when we came home and found it abandoned, and it was snapped up in less than half an hour. Rooms are hard to come by whenever there is a festival."

"So I understand," Albert remarked as he moved inside the house.

Rex was sniffing the air once more, already finding the distinct scents of the couple he'd first met in Arbroath.

"They were here all right," he reported to his human even though the old man was talking to the landlady and wouldn't understand him. "I can smell the vineyard too. They came back here after they were there. I can smell the soil."

Rex announced his findings with a slow wag of his tail. They were on the trail of two criminals, and he liked that. He wasn't entirely sure what they had done – the concept of theft was not one a dog could understand, but from Millie and Thor, he knew a man had died and some others had vanished. He would aid his human to track them and hoped there might be a game of chase and bite in the offing.

Alice led Albert through the house and up some stairs to the second floor. Using a key, she opened a door marked at head height with a large brass number seven and walked inside.

"You say the couple staying here might have been involved in some kind of criminal caper?" Alice was playing down her interest, making her question sound more casual than it was, but it came as no surprise to Albert. A life as a police detective had proven that most folks found the idea of criminals quite intriguing. Not that they would want to welcome them into their house or offer their daughter's hand in marriage, but having an unusual anecdote up one's sleeve …

Albert paused just inside the door to the guestroom, drinking in the room with his eyes first. Over his shoulder he answered Alice's question.

"I believe that to be the case. If you will allow me a few

moments, I am going to have a thorough look around their room and then I will have some questions for you."

Alice worried, "You're not going to make a mess, are you? I've only just finished making the room up with fresh bedding."

Albert promised he would put everything back as it was and unclipped Rex's lead. If asked why he set his dog loose, Albert would have struggled to articulate his thoughts, but it was mostly to do with the belief that Rex was somehow involved in the investigation too. Though Albert was unable to understand what his dog was doing or interpret to any worthwhile degree his actions or the sounds he made, Albert could not help but conclude that Rex was working alongside him.

Letting him off the lead to sniff around just made sense.

Free to roam, Rex chose to remain sitting where he was when his human went into the room. He could smell this was where the couple from Arbroath had been staying – their individual scents lingered even though they were now masked by the odour of cleaning products.

Closing his eyes to filter out a weaker sense, Rex concentrated on what he could smell. There was the unmistakable saltiness of the beach, but he dismissed that because everywhere and everything in Whitstable carried the same smell. Hard to detect, but there nonetheless, was the smell of the sausage factory in Reculver and lurking in the background was the unmistakable blend of earthy notes from the vineyard in Eccles.

Albert wished he could have gotten to the bed and breakfast sooner, before Alice had the chance to clean it. He looked around, getting down on his knees to check under the bed even though Alice assured him she had cleaned the room thoroughly when she saw what he was doing.

The closet and drawers were empty. There was nothing in the wastepaper basket.

"Was there anything to throw out?" Albert asked, pointing to the small plastic bin with its fresh, scented, plastic bag liner.

Alice hadn't expected the question. "Oh, um. A few things. A couple of cotton buds covered in earwax if I remember correctly and maybe a makeup wipe or two."

Hardly the stuff that would blow a case wide open.

Albert asked, "Would you be able to find it?" He assumed the plastic bag lining the bin was removed and the contents went with it each day or upon changeover of residents.

Alice really hadn't expected that question. "Whatever for?"

"To be thorough, Alice. To be thorough. I may be entirely wrong about the couple who were staying here, but if I am right then they need to be caught."

Clearly not happy about the task and thinking now she ought not to have agreed to let Albert in, Alice wrinkled her nose and questioned how far down the bin outside the small bag from this room might be.

"I guess I can show you where to look," she ventured, hoping she could hand the task back.

Albert nodded. "Good enough."

Rex chose that moment to go into the room. There was another smell, a really faint one that he was trying and failing to pinpoint.

"He won't make a mess, will he?" Alice questioned, voicing her concern for a second time.

Albert chose to not answer, watching Rex instead as he padded across the carpet and sniffed at a spot near the chest of drawers.

Rex tensed when he worked out what he could smell and was about to bark when he changed his mind. The smell – one he'd been trained to react to – was so faint it was almost not there. Even if he could get his message across, what would his human do? There was nothing for Rex to show him.

Choosing to file the information away and wait to see if it became pertinent, Rex looked up at Albert, gave a wag of his tail and raised his eyebrows.

"Are you done? I'm done." Rex said, intoning the message with his eyes.

Unable to understand, Albert asked, "Are you done, boy?"

Rex rolled his eyes and left the room, strolling out past Alice to wait at the top of the stairs.

Having struck out with the room, Albert switched to asking questions.

"Did you have much chance to talk with Suzie and Nathan?"

"Not really, Albert. A few words in passing, but they mostly kept to themselves. They were polite, please don't misunderstand me – I got nothing from them that might suggest they were anything other than what they said they were."

"They had a car, yes?"

"Yes." Alice thought it was rather an odd question. What sort of person travelled without a car these days? "It was a nice BMW. A five series, I think. Black." She showed off her memory skills.

"You wouldn't happen to know the registration number, would you?"

He had her there. "Not off the top of my head. But I log all the registration numbers when people arrive – parking can be terrible around here at peak times, so I want to always make sure the cars outside are those of my residents. We had a bit of a war with the neighbours a year ago."

Reaching the bottom of the stairs, Alice bustled off to the kitchen where she found her notebook.

"Here it is." She showed Albert the entry where she'd written the number and letter combination against the names of her guests. "Here's a funny thing," Alice led into what she wanted to say next while Albert copied the registration number into his phone. "I heard him call his wife Tanya instead of Suzie."

Albert's eyes flared – this could be a huge lead!

"Definitely Tanya?" he questioned, wanting to see how certain she might be.

"Oh, yes. It was more than once, actually. I didn't say anything, of course, but I saw her slap him on the arm the second time. I thought maybe they were having an affair and were staying here under false names. Then I remembered I'd seen both their IDs – their names really are Suzie and Nathan Davis. What do you think the Tanya thing was about?"

Albert had a darned good idea. He was willing to bet Tanya was her real name. The couple had good fake identification and credit cards to complete the picture, but her accomplice sounded like an idiot. Thinking back, Albert remembered how odd the couple had acted at times in Arbroath. It hadn't registered at the time – he'd been too busy trying to solve a mystery to really notice.

To avoid getting into a lengthy explanation, Albert said, "I believe they were using fake names and rather expensive identification to match." Then, because they were already on the subject of Alice overhearing other people's conversations, he asked, "Did you hear what they were talking about at any point? Did they mention Reculver, or did you ever hear them say the name Camilla Humphries-Bowden?"

Alice made a surprised face, but gave the question some consideration before answering.

While the humans were talking, Rex chose to explore the kitchen. He could smell Hobnob biscuits among other things and there were interesting smells coming from under the sink where he could tell a waste food receptacle was placed. Bacon fat was the dominant smell invading his brain.

He nudged at the door with his nose, hoping it might spring open and that the bacon would attack his face. That way he would be able to claim self-defence when he ate it all.

The door didn't budge.

"I don't recall them saying anything about Reculver," Alice remarked, her eyes fixed on nothing at all as she consulted her memory. "I'm not sure about Camilla either, though ..." Alice took a step to her left which brought the back door into reach. Opening it a foot, she leaned her head out. "GLEN!"

Her bellow was answered a second later by an unseen man.

"Yes, love?" The tone of his reply was that of a husband who wasn't sure why his name was being yelled and worried it might be because he had done something wrong. Or forgotten to do something. Or merely been outside pottering in the shed for too long.

"Have you got a minute?" Alice shouted back.

A few seconds later, a man in a dark green quilted body warmer over a white cotton shirt and brown corduroy trousers appeared at the back door. His cheeks were ruddy from the cool air outside.

"Hello?" he said his greeting as a question, unsure who the man in his kitchen might be or why it would result in him being summoned.

Alice dealt with the introduction as Albert extended his right hand.

"Glen this is Albert. I told you about him earlier."

"Oh, yes. The investigator." The two men shook hands and let their arms fall back to their sides. Neither spoke, each expecting Alice to carry on with what she was saying.

"Albert was asking questions about the couple who absconded last night. Did you hear them talking about Reculver? Or about …." Alice looked to Albert for him to remind her of the name.

"Camilla Humphries-Bowden," he supplied.

Much like his wife, Glen gave the question some thought, but his conclusion was no different.

"No. No, I'm afraid not."

Albert pursed his lips in disappointment. "How about Leon Harold? Does that name ring any bells?"

Glen and Alice looked inward at each other, but drew a blank there too.

"They talked about oysters a lot," volunteered Glen.

Rex's ears pricked up.

"Oysters?" Albert hadn't once thought about a possible connection to Whitstable's most famous product. The Gastrothief was all about food, that his agents were here to rob one of the oyster houses ought to have been obvious. Which one though?

"Yes. The chap, Nathan, he …"

Glen was cut off by Alice speaking. "That's not his real name."

Glen blinked a couple of times, his mouth still open with the words he was going to say poised on the tip of his tongue. Pushing them to one side, he asked the obvious question.

"Really? What's his real name then?"

Albert admitted the truth. "That I don't know, but Suzie and Nathan Davis don't exist. Her name is probably Tanya, I have just learned." Albert remarked, making a mental note to make sure he passed that on to Gary when he made the call about the car.

Steering Glen back to what he had been saying, Albert said, "You were telling me about Nathan and the oysters?"

Glen needed a second to retrace the thread of what he'd been attempting to say, but once his brain caught up, he launched back into the story.

"Yes, that's right. Well, Nathan or whatever his name is, he had a tide timetable. You know, one of those charts they make that shows when the high and low tides will occur on any given day of the year."

You couldn't tell by looking at Albert's face, but much like the serene swan, his brain was working like the blazes under the surface. Oysters and tides? What connected them? The Gastrothief couldn't want his agents to collect the oysters straight from the beds at low tide – that would be too time consuming, and someone would catch them.

The Gastrothief wanted a truck full of Stilton cheese. He stole equipment and people so the foods he was after could be produced at his leisure. He couldn't do that by collecting some oysters from the sea. They wouldn't keep.

It had to be something else. But what?

Rex nudged Albert's leg. "Ask them if there is any food they don't need. I think better on a full stomach."

Albert scratched Rex's head with a free hand, his brain whirring too fast for him to pay his dog any attention.

The doorbell chimed, getting Alice's attention. She started to move, but paused to touch Glen's arm.

"Albert was asking about the rubbish bag I took out of their room. He thinks there could be a clue in it."

Glen's eyes filled with mischievous excitement. "How thrilling," he gasped.

Whoever was outside rang the doorbell again, the insistent noise prompting Alice to get moving. Over her shoulder she gave her husband instructions.

"I need you to go to the supermarket, dear. We're running low on milk, and you should get some of the good biscuits while you are there."

"What about the rubbish for Albert?" he queried.

In a tone that left no doubt she thought his question asinine, Alice replied, "Do that first. Obviously." Muttering under her breath, she continued to the door, leaving both men and the dog in the kitchen.

Albert looked at Glen expectantly.

Rex copied him, but said, "Anything will do so long as it's food. I'm not fussy."

Backing away, Glen hooked a thumb toward the door. "The bins are outside."

17

DUMPSTER DIVING

Albert made a call to his son, Gary, while following Glen around the building to find the bins. Gary answered almost instantly and listened when Albert passed on the vehicle registration number and the new name he'd uncovered.

It wasn't a whole lot to go on, especially since Tanya was a fairly common name, but it was more than they'd had before, and each new clue brought them just a little bit closer to figuring out the truth.

Gary promised to look into the car. Unless the number plate was completely fake, they would find it.

Albert put the phone back in his pocket just as they rounded a corner.

The bin turned out to be one of those giant roll top things.

"It'll be in this corner," Glen pointed to where he meant, and peered inside.

Excited by the smells seeping out now the lid was open, Rex jumped up, placing his front paws on the bin to get his nose closer.

"We're going dumpster diving?" he enquired with an excited wag of his tail. "This is brilliant! You're always telling me off for nosing around the bins. I'm not sure what has caused the change of heart, but I like it."

Albert shoved against Rex's shoulder. "Get down, Rex."

Knocked off balance, Rex let his front paws fall back to the ground and glared at his human.

"What is going on?" he wanted to know. The human who lived here had opened the giant bin and then left them looking into it. He hadn't gone far though and Rex could already see him returning with a small stepladder.

"This will make getting in and out a tad easier," Glen announced, unfolding the steps and placing them at the mouth of the roll-top bin. "I'm a little too old to be vaulting in and out as I might have done a few decades ago."

Albert nodded his agreement. He could remember being young and athletic. He could remember being a fast runner and having the kind of figure that made him happy to take his shirt off at the beach on a sunny day. He could remember, but only just.

Glen climbed a few steps and carefully swung a leg into the three-quarters filled receptacle. The surface was unstable, the thin, black plastic bags inside crushing under his weight. He kept one hand on the mouth of the bin as he attempted to take a step.

Unwilling to let the man go it alone, Albert followed him up and in.

Rex wagged his tail "Right, I see. You're a good friend, old man, you know that? You're going in there to find the best bits for me. I'll just wait then."

Albert and Glen were doing their best to keep their balance as the trash continued to compact beneath their feet. The smell coming off the waste was ripe and unpleasant, but Glen believed he knew precisely which bag he needed.

"It'll be this one here," he claimed with confidence, selecting a black sack that looked exactly the same as all the other black sacks. It was in the far corner where Glen stated he threw it just an hour ago.

However, his certainty proved to be unwarranted. The bag contained general household waste such as empty packets and vegetable peelings. The small bags Alice collected from the guest bedrooms this morning were not within.

Now sounding less sure of himself, Glen pointed to the opposite corner. "Perhaps I threw it there instead."

The second attempt drew a blank too.

Rex's paws were becoming agitated in his impatience. The smells wafting out of the bin as the men stomped the trash down and forced the air inside the bags out was driving him crazy. Somewhere in there was a half-eaten burger, some pizza still in its box and a Chinese takeaway from two days ago.

Glen tried another bag and then another, his guesses proving fruitless each time.

Albert had gone through the point where he regretted climbing in after Glen and was starting to worry that he'd been in the bin long enough that the smell might be starting to permeate his clothing.

He wanted to find the rubbish from Suzie and Nathan's room, but the chances were that it would contain nothing of any use. Delving into the contents of any more bin bags was a level of dedication he refused to achieve, but turning to wade back to the stepladder through the split and opened bags, he noticed that Rex was no longer sitting where he had been.

Albert got a half second of warning – just enough time for an expletive to form on his lips.

Rex, bored of waiting, hungry because he'd gorged himself, vomited, and then missed his dinner, and only too happy to muck in as the humans looked for the good food hidden in the depths of the bin, had chosen to join them.

He'd backed up a few yards, started running, and leapt into the air. His human chose that moment to look up, but rather than congratulate Rex for his willingness to help, the old man looked angry.

Albert fell backward to get out of the way as Rex landed, all four paws sinking instantly through the supposed surface of the bags. Three of his paws punctured bags which further added to the smell and amount of loose garbage.

Albert cried out in horror. "Arrrrrgh! No, Rex!"

Rex wagged his tail, ducking his head into a gap when his nose led him there. He popped back out a moment later with a slice of pizza between his teeth.

Rex barked, "Ta-dah!" It came out a little garbled through his pizza filled mouth, but there was no hiding the triumph he felt.

Albert grabbed the piece of pizza still poking out of Rex's mouth.

"Give me that, you horrible dog!"

Rex bit down hard, unwilling to give up his prize.

"There's more in here, you know. This bit is mine. If your nose worked better, you'd have found it first."

The half in Albert's hand ripped free, sending him tumbling backward in the stinking trash again.

"I've found it!" announced Glen, holding a bag aloft.

Rex scoffed the pizza in his mouth and watched in horror as the old man threw the piece he had into an open black bin and held it out of the way.

"Oi! If you don't want it, why are you taking it from me?"

Albert hooked Rex's collar, hauling his head around before the dog could find anything else to eat.

"You'll make yourself sick again, you daft dog. That pizza could have been in here for days!"

"It's last night's, actually," supplied Glen, helpfully. "The couple staying in room five ordered it."

"See?" complained Rex, fighting against Albert to get back to the pizza box.

Albert held on tight and thought it a mercy the dog had nothing to push against.

"I'm going to need a hand getting him out," he begged of Glen.

Seeing the truth of the predicament, Glen dropped the bag he held over the side and made his way to the step ladder. Between them and with Rex battling to go the other way, they got the heavy German Shepherd to the edge of the bin.

"Now what?" panted Glen, out of breath.

The level of the rubbish in the bin had dropped three feet in the last few minutes as they trampled it down. Getting Rex out now required them to bodily lift him to head height and neither man was up to that.

With a sigh, Albert said, "I'll get you fish and chips for lunch if you get yourself out, Rex."

Rex stared at his human, listening intently for the catch. When none came and the old man repeated his offer with an insistent motion, Rex leapt onto the lip of the bin and down again, spinning in excited circles as his mouth began to water.

"Oh, my goodness! What are you two doing?" demanded Alice, hanging out of the kitchen door to see what was taking Glen so long. Then the smell hit her, and she covered her mouth and nose. "Oh, dear Lord, you stink!"

"We're getting fish and chips for lunch!" barked Rex.

Glen held the stepladder steady for Albert to clamber out and down, observing the rather worrying damp and sticky patches on Albert's clothing and seeing much the same on his own.

"We were looking for the rubbish bag, love," Glen explained.

Peeking through a gap between the door and frame, Alice said, "Well you're not coming in the house smelling like that. You can jolly well strip those clothes off in the shed. I'll bring out a bucket and some soap."

Albert sniffed at the sleeve of his coat. He could detect a vague odour, but questioned whether it might be worse than he thought – he'd been in the bin for the last few minutes and perhaps his nose was used to it now.

"Um, I could do with getting cleaned up too."

Alice's eyes flared. "I'm afraid not, Mr Smith. I've been more than generous with my time today. You can come back at any time when you do not stink like a garbage heap."

Feeling a little stuck now, Albert asked, "I need to find some accommodation in the area. I don't suppose you would know of anywhere that might have a room?"

"Ha!" Alice scoffed. "Like I told you earlier, Albert, it's the festival this weekend. There's not a room to be had anywhere. No one would let you in even if they did though, not smelling like that."

Sensing he was done at the bed and breakfast, Albert thanked Alice and Glen for their help, wished Glen luck getting clean in the shed, and picked through the contents of the trash from Suzie and Nathan's room. There was nothing to find.

It really had been nothing more than a few makeup wipes and some cotton buds covered in ear wax. Just as he was about to discard the bag, he spotted one other item. It was a small triangle of blue paper, about three quarters of an inch long on each side. Two sides were sharply cut and the third was rough, like it had been torn – it was the corner of something.

Albert turned the bag over to find the blue paper was white on the other side. There were no markings on either side save for a small pattern on the blue side right on the edge of the tear.

It was nothing, he decided. He'd wasted more time and got himself covered in filth for a bag containing trash. Accepting that not every lead led to a clue, he acknowledged that the visit hadn't been a waste of time - he'd learned about oysters and tide times. Those were worthwhile clues. And he'd gained a name: Tanya. That was something he could use.

A check of his watch revealed that lunch ought to be over for Roy and Beverly and at just that moment his phone rang. Dumping the clear plastic bag back into the rolltop bin, he thumbed the green button to answer the call.

18

DIRTY OLD MAN

"Where are you, old boy?" asked Roy. They were finished with lunch and heading for the fish market. Roy had elected to check in with his friend first.

"I'm just heading back towards the carpark. Is there any chance I can get my bags? I could do with a change of clothes."

Albert did his best to explain why he needed to swap out what he was wearing, but the Hope's got the message in all its glory when he arrived back at the car to discover they were downwind from him.

"Golly, that's a bit ripe, old bean," Roy reported though the words came out sounding quite nasal because like his wife he was holding his nose.

Albert sniffed his coat again.

"Really? It's that bad?"

Roy nodded vigorously and Beverly retreated several yards, plipping the car open with her remote.

"You'll need more than a change of clothes, Albert," she shouted from a safe distance. "You're going to need to get a wash too."

"She might be right, old chap," Roy agreed.

With the car's boot lid open, Albert rummaged around to find a suitable change of clothing and his washbag. He didn't have a towel but determined he could just make do. There were public restrooms along the beach where he would find warm water and a place to get changed. It was far from ideal, but he wasn't seeing a lot of options.

With his backpack filled with the things he needed and a plastic shopping bag from Beverly's collection in the boot to put his dirty clothes in, Albert waved the couple goodbye and promised to meet them again shortly.

Rex skipped along merrily at the end of his lead, making his way back to the fish and chip place where Albert promised he would fulfil his bargain.

Albert and Rex took the same back streets as the previous night to return to the fish and chip place. Exiting the narrow passage onto the seaside resort's main thoroughfare, Albert turned right and walked straight into the chip shop.

The complaints began immediately.

Joining the back of a short queue of people waiting to order takeaway fish and chips, it took about two seconds before the first nose wrinkled and the person in front turned around.

"Oh, my goodness, you stink!" complained a woman in her thirties surrounded by a gaggle of children.

From behind the counter, another woman arrowed an arm toward the door.

"This isn't a homeless shelter. You need to leave."

"I'm not homeless," Albert protested. Every eye in the place was staring at him in disgust. "I, ah, I had a little accident is all."

The woman behind the counter was dismissive in her response. "Whatever. I'm not serving you smelling like that. There's dirt in your hair!"

Automatically, Albert reached up to touch his hair, but stopped his hand halfway. He clearly smelled far worse than he believed, and there seemed little to be gained by arguing.

With a nod of his head, he backed toward the door, getting a gasp of horror as a couple attempting to come through it caught sight and smell of him.

Rex held firm. "What about the fish and chips?" he wanted to know. "I'm hungry."

Albert gave the lead a tug. "We'll come back shortly, boy." He was forced to drag Rex from the shop, the dog doing his best to make himself heavy and trying hard to dig his claws into the tiled floor.

Far from happy, Rex sulked all the way to the beach and the public restrooms.

It wasn't even close to being warm enough inside for Albert to be happy about taking off his clothes. The restroom looked to have been built at the turn of the previous century and long before people thought about adding conveniences such as heating. Worse yet the door was jammed open, and he couldn't get it to budge, so the cold air blowing in off the beach was coming straight inside.

Muttering under his breath to no one but himself. Albert ran the hot water – which was more accurately described as warm - chained Rex to a convenient pipe, and peeled off his coat, jumper, and shirt.

Standing in just a vest, the cold air instantly nipping at his skin, Albert shed his shoes, trousers, and socks. The floor was far too cold for his feet, necessitating the use of his jumper to act as a barrier.

Then, with Rex eying him curiously, Albert started to wash himself. To his way of thinking, the smell ought to be restricted to his clothing – very little of his flesh had come into contact with the rubbish and dirt in the bin, but for thoroughness, he scrubbed as much of his skin as he could access without taking off another layer.

He was about done when he heard voices approaching. Still standing in his vest and underpants, he thought it a little cruel for the world to throw an extra dimension onto his woes. Trying to dry himself quickly with the clean vest he'd selected for the task, he realised the voices he could hear approaching belonged to ladies, not men.

He breathed a sigh of relief and locking eyes with Rex, made a show of wiping his brow. Then his eyes caught the sign on the face of the door he'd been unable to close, and his heart stopped beating.

In his haste, he'd somehow managed to walk into the ladies'

toilet by mistake. With eyes on stalks and his brain desperately calculating whether he could dart into a stall and hide before they found him in his state of undress, he spotted the coin operated sanitary towel dispenser on the wall and the utter lack of urinals anywhere in sight.

Too late, the approaching voices came through the door and stopped dead.

Gawping in horror at the mostly naked man staring back at her, Kimberly Bryant, in Whitstable for a weekend break with three colleagues from work, felt Sophie bump into her. Kimberly had stopped moving, blocking her friend's access to the toilets while her feet and bladder argued.

She really needed to pee, but there was no chance she was going in here now.

About to ask what was happening, Sophie spotted Albert and screamed. The sudden blast of sound so close to her head jolted Kimberly and she screamed too.

Startled by the noise, and wondering if there was something he needed to do, Rex jumped to his feet. He did it with his usual exuberance and consequently snapped the pipe Albert chose to loop his lead around.

The women ran from the restroom, screaming still and yelling about dirty old men as water under pressure shot skyward.

Unable to believe his luck, Albert snatched up his backpack of clean clothing before the jet of water could soak it.

Free of his tether, Rex was backing away. He didn't mind going for a swim, but he wasn't volunteering to get wet for any other reason or by any other method.

Trailing expletives as he went, Albert clutched the bag of dirty clothes to his chest, hooked his backpack over one shoulder and leaving his jumper in a growing pool of water, ran from the ladies' restroom.

Out of the restroom, around to the right and back in through another door – this one displaying the universal sign for a man – Albert streaked in his underwear, the cold and pieces of loose gravel both biting into his feet all the way.

Thanking the Lord for small mercies he found the mens' room to be empty. To cap things off the door wasn't jammed like the ladies' had been.

Just a couple of minutes later, Albert straightened his outfit, practiced his innocent expression in the mirror, and braved the outside world again. He didn't have a spare coat so was instantly cold, not that he'd been warm at any point in the last ten minutes, but resolved to buy a new one at a shop in town.

The clean up wasn't done yet though. Rex still stank to high heaven and now that Albert was fresh and clean, he could smell it. People had been right to complain. He would have too.

"Fish and chips now?" asked Rex, wagging his tail. There was a lot of confusing stuff happening, and an investigation the old man was still pursuing, yet none of that negated the need to eat.

Albert knew Rex wouldn't willingly go into the sea, but with a quick trip to a chip shop – a different one than before, and he left Rex tied to a lamppost outside – he believed he could get the dog smelling significantly better than he currently did.

Rex trailed after the warm bag of fish and chips, nudging Albert's arm every few yards because he couldn't see a good reason why they were not already devouring the contents. At the beach, he expected his human to unwrap the parcel, which he did, Rex sitting obediently at his human's feet.

However, expecting a handful of chips to be tossed into the air, Rex was surprised to see the old man's arm going behind his head as he prepared to throw them.

Mesmerised by the greasy morsels, he ran after them, his eyes only on the tasty treats. As gravity sucked them back toward the earth, Rex leapt, his mouth open to snatch the chips from the sky. His teeth closed around the deep-fried tubers and his paws hit the water.

Luckily for Rex, the water wasn't so deep that his head went under, but Albert had aimed his throw with enough accuracy to land Rex in seawater up to his shoulders.

Rex didn't care. There were chips. There was fish. His human wanted to play a game and that was fine by him.

Albert repeated the throw six times, deciding Rex was as soggy as he would get by then. He also knew Rex well enough to be certain his dog would run along the beach now and find one of the sandy spots to roll on. A trip to the beach always did wonders for Rex's coat, removing grime and grease and whatever else got into it. Once he was dry, a good brushing would take out a whole stack of loose hair to leave him looking glossy.

All Albert cared about was getting rid of the smell. He set the rest of the fish and chips on the pebbles for Rex to consume and stared at the sea where it lapped the shore. What were the Gastrothief's agents up to? What did they have planned?

19

INTRUDER ALERT!

Beverly declared Albert's refreshed condition acceptable. He'd chosen to discard his smelly clothes, something he wouldn't have done if he was going home and could use his own washing machine. Travelling for almost two months, he'd made use of various B&B owners' generosity to get his things laundered and pressed. He doubted anyone would be pleased to receive that which he had just left in a public rubbish bin.

A replacement coat came from a charity shop where it had adorned a mannequin in the window. The price tag on it was less than he would pay for a pint of beer, so he'd given them a tenner and told them to keep the change.

Together with Roy and Beverly, Albert and Rex were leaving Whitstable, heading a short distance down the coast to another seaside resort. Albert hadn't visited Sandwich in years, but knew it to be one of those medieval towns that had been in the same spot for hundreds and hundreds of years. He remembered that it still had ancient fortifications around the town that were erected centuries ago to defend against foreign invaders.

They didn't get as far as the town though. The address Albert had for Camilla Humphries-Bowden was a mile short, sitting hidden from view by rows of trees that had clearly been planted a long time ago.

"This is the address you have for her?" Beverly questioned, angling her car into a long driveway.

They were approaching a large house set in its own grounds. There was no danger of ever having to worry the neighbour's kids might play their music too loud – there wasn't another house in sight.

Albert double checked, but they were in the right place.

Parking right in front of the large front door, Beverly announced her intention to stay in the car.

"Will you be quick, Albert? I've bought fresh fish and I don't want to leave it too long before I get it home."

"We'll be as swift as possible, my dear," replied Roy, unclipping his seatbelt, and twisting to get his door handle.

Beverly placed a hand on his leg.

"Where do you think you're going, Roy? Albert doesn't need any help. Do you, Albert?" she asked pointedly.

Albert was more than happy to have his friend tag along, he quite liked having a human companion around. He loved Rex with all his heart, but having someone to talk to who could answer back … well, it just added a certain something.

However, Beverly had asked him a question and the honest answer was a simple one to give.

"No, probably not. I'm just going to check on her and see if I can glean a little more information about who she thinks might have been following her. If she is the target, they will be coming for her soon." Albert was certain Tanya and her male companion – he chose to continue referring to him as Nathan for the time being - would want to finish their business here and make good their escape. They certainly hadn't hung around after they saw him last night. "We might be able to set a trap," he added.

Beverly arched her eyebrows. "You mean to use a young woman as bait?"

Albert had his hand on the handle of the car door, but stopped moving to consider Beverly's accusation.

"Not exactly," he managed. Seeing he hadn't convinced Roy's wife, he tried again. "Look, no one believes the Gastrothief exists. If it weren't for the fact that I have three children in high-ranking positions in the police, I would be nowhere with this at all. But their hands are tied too. They cannot do anything more than they have because there just isn't any proof. All I have is speculation to link crimes from right across the country that go back months. I need something concrete, and the Gastrothief's agents coming after Camilla could be it. She won't be in any danger. If I think she is the target, and honestly, I already do, then I will make sure she has protection."

Opting to exit the car before Beverly could level another question, Albert had Rex right on his tail. As he swung the door shut, he caught Beverly observing in horror that the back seat was now covered in sand where Rex had been lying.

Crossing the gravel drive with hurried steps, Albert pressed the buzzer and employed the knocker too for good measure.

It was answered in less than two seconds, surprising Albert who expected to have to ring the bell again.

"Goodness," he exclaimed upon seeing a young woman he assumed to be Camilla. "Were you hiding behind the door?"

The young woman, wearing heels and a fitted dress that looked expensive and was office chic rather than designed for an evening out, tilted her head to one side, eyeing Albert curiously.

"I saw you pull up?" she pointed to the doorbell. "It's connected to my phone. I wouldn't have answered the door otherwise. Are you Albert Smith?"

Rex wagged his tail and barked.

Albert stuck out his hand. "Yes. Sorry. You caught me by surprise there. I am Albert and this is Rex. Am I addressing Camilla?"

"Sorry, yes." It was a conversation of apologies. "Please come in." Camilla stepped back to allow her guests entry, but craned her head to look at the people still sitting in the car outside her door.

"Are your friends not coming in?"

Albert removed his coat. "It would seem not."

With the door closed and the cool air of late autumn shut outside once more, Albert got down to business.

"You live alone, Camilla?"

"Oh, goodness, no. I live with ma and pa, but they are on a cruise. You're going to tell me I'm exposed living out here in the middle of nowhere, aren't you?"

Albert pulled a face that agreed with her point.

"Yes, I thought as much," Camilla replied, her voice quiet and a little sad.

Aiming to give her some reassurance, but really hoping he could extract information from her, he licked his lips and got ready to gently interview her. She thought someone was watching her or following her and Albert believed her one hundred percent.

Choosing a tactful approach because he didn't wish to scare her, Albert said, "Cam …"

The rest of his sentence was cut off by someone hammering at the door.

Camilla jumped, snatching up her phone so she could activate the doorbell camera app and see who was there.

There was no need.

"Albert! Albert, old boy. There's an intruder on the grounds!" Roy's voice, muffled by the door, echoed through the house when he shouted, nonetheless.

Albert darted to a window, looking out at the lawn and trees beyond. Roy wasn't given to fanciful notions, so if he believed there was someone out there, then there was.

To Camilla, Albert snapped, "Call the police! Tell them who you are and where you are and that the persons responsible for the fire at the Porker factory in Reculver are cornered here." To himself he muttered, "That will get them moving."

Camilla was freaking out. She had her phone out, but couldn't operate it. Her hands were shaking, and she was babbling incoherent nonsense about living a better life if God would just help her to not get killed by some wine hating maniac.

Roy thumped the door again, shouting to be heard.

Albert needed to get to him – if Tanya and Nathan heard the

shouts of alarm, they might scarper and that would end his chance to catch them. First though, he had to calm Camilla.

Taking her shoulders in his hands, he gave them a firm squeeze.

"You are not alone, Camilla. Nothing is going to happen to you. Rex is a former police dog. If anyone is here, he will chase them off."

Rex wagged his tail when Camilla flicked her eyes in his direction.

"Call the police, Camilla, but tell them to come without sirens. We want to catch these people if possible, not scare them off."

Beverly's voice joined Roy's "Let us in!"

Camilla looked up at Albert, her eyes filled with the hope that she could trust him.

"You said they killed Simon Major," she argued.

Albert shook his head. "No, I said Simon Major died. I believe they intended to kidnap him."

Camilla cried, "Why?"

"I'll explain soon, I promise. Just rest assured that murder is not their intention."

Beverly started kicking the front door. "Let us in! There are mad killers out here, Albert!"

"Mad killers!" Camilla gibbered, her eyes as wide as saucers. "She said they are mad killers!"

Huffing with frustration, Albert yet again begged Camilla to call the police – the fear in her voice would be enough to make the dispatcher light a fire under any units in the area. They would get here fast.

Heading for the door, Albert fired a command at Rex.

"Rex, guard the lady!"

Instantly, Rex's back end came off the floor and his hackle rose as he shifted posture both mentally and physically. He was ready to defend against anyone who might try to attack.

Beverly tumbled through the door when Albert opened it. Roy was standing a few yards away, staring into the distance at something. Albert couldn't spot what it was and beckoned for Roy to come inside.

"There's someone out there, old boy," Roy reinforced the claim he'd been bellowing through the door and brandished his walking cane like a sword once more. "I spotted the bounder coming over the boundary hedge, wot."

Albert got Roy inside and pushed the door so it was almost closed. Then he peered out.

"Where?"

Roy, crammed in next to Albert, raised his walking cane to point out a spot across the impressive grounds. On the other side of a meadow, a high hedgerow marked what he assumed to be the edge of the property.

"Over there, old boy. Looked like a man. Tall one too though he was moving cautiously like a fellow who didn't want anyone to spot him."

Albert pushed back and closed the door. He could hear Beverly talking to the police and guessed she had taken over from Camilla. Whether Camilla had asked her to remained to be seen – Albert had forgotten how bossy Roy's wife could be.

Arriving in the kitchen, Albert caught Beverly's last line.

"… and you need to get here right now, or we'll all be dead!"

Camilla had a tear on her left cheek and was wringing her hands together with worry. She was facing Beverly, letting the older woman do the talking. Albert believed the danger had been exaggerated, but since his desire was to bring the police in as great a number as possible, it was entirely possible Beverly's panicked claims would do the trick.

"That's what I said!" she blurted in reply to a question no one else heard. "It's the same ones who burnt down the Porker factory yesterday." Clearly the police dispatcher at the other end said something else because Beverly was listening for once. Her eyes darted about, fixing on nothing, until the other person fell silent once more. Then she placed her hand over the phone's mouthpiece and looked at Albert. "He wants to know how we know who it is."

Albert motioned for her to hand over the mobile phone, then in a calm voice addressed the police dispatcher.

"This is retired Detective Superintendent Smith. Please inform

Chief Inspector Quinn of Kent police that the Reculver arsonists are here and that he will need to hurry if he is to catch them." Albert then thumbed the red button to end the call, confident that the dispatcher would not dare to do anything other than exactly as he had asked.

Handing the phone to Camilla, he said, "They will most likely call back, attempting to get more information and to confirm we are okay. Do not answer it. They will move faster if we keep them in the dark."

He was about to say something else, planning to quiz Roy for more detail on the figure he'd seen, but a door slammed shut somewhere deep inside the house and everyone froze.

20

YOU'RE ALL MAD!

Camilla squeaked a rude word, blushing with embarrassment at her slip, then gasped, "That was the back door that leads off the kitchen. I didn't think to lock it."

Rex took a step toward the direction the sound came from, twisting his head to glance at his human. *Was it time to play chase and bite?*

Albert stooped to pick up Rex's lead, wrapping it tightly around his right wrist to be sure he had a good grip.

"What do we do?" whispered Beverly. "Shouldn't we get in the car and drive home really fast? I've got fresh fish in the boot," she explained unnecessarily.

Roy brandished his walking cane again. "I say we teach the blighter a lesson, wot."

Beverly slapped his arm. "Don't be such an idiot, Roy Hope. You're seventy-seven."

Albert frowned, trying to listen and unable to hear because of all the chatter. Had it been the wind blowing the door shut or had someone come inside? If they were trying to sneak up on Camilla, surely they would want their entrance to be as quiet as possible.

"Beverly might be right. Perhaps you should go. No sense in us all staying here. The police will be along shortly; you can wait by the gate and follow them back in when it's safe."

Beverly grabbed her car keys, but Roy said, "If you're staying, old boy, then you'll find me at your side."

"You men are mad," remarked Beverly, heading for the door. "Come along, Camilla."

Albert spun around to deliver his next comment. "No, Camilla has to stay!" Faced with questioning and confused expressions, Albert explained, "If they see her go, they will leave and will have escaped before the police arrive."

Beverly threw her arms in the air. "So? So what? If she leaves now, they can't get her."

Albert locked eyes with Camilla. "Until they come back."

His words were enough to make her gulp, but she nodded her head. "He's right. I've felt like there was someone following me for a week or more now. If we can catch them now, maybe this can be over. Even if I have to be the bait, I think it's worth a shot."

Beverly couldn't believe her ears. "You're all mad."

The sound of a door hinge squeaking silenced them all again and Rex strained against his lead. He wanted to go. There was a person to take down and he was the right dog for the job.

Albert was in two minds about whether to let Rex go or not. He believed the Gastrothief's agents were dangerous career criminals. Capable of kidnap, murder, and all manner of other crimes, he expected them to be armed and to feel no compunction about harming Rex or worse.

They were here for Camilla, but did they know she wasn't alone? Probably, he decided. They would have been watching the property and saw Beverly's car when it arrived. With a jolt, Albert realised they had probably seen him and Rex, and it prompted their decision to move.

They knew who he was, and after running into him yesterday, must believe he was here to cause them problems. It was why they were at his house this morning. He was now as much their target as Camilla.

A ball of worry filled Albert's stomach, fear gripping him until he recognised it for what it was and forced it away.

The man and the woman, Tanya and whatever his real name happened to be, were in the house and coming for him. Well, he wasn't going to wait for them to find him.

Crouching to put his head alongside Rex's he whispered, "Stay quiet, boy. We're taking the fight to them." All he had in his arsenal was the element of surprise. That and a large dog, of course. If he found them and could catch them off guard, maybe Rex could take them both down. Rex would certainly get one, leaving just one for him to tackle. Albert picked up a brass candlestick, hefting it in his right hand and feeling more confident for it.

The police would be here soon. The words echoed in his head as he set off.

Urgent whispering ensued instantly – Beverly still felt running away was the only sensible policy to employ and was trying to take Roy and Camilla with her. Roy was having none of it and Camilla chose to follow Albert which sealed the deal. Soon, all three of them were tracking along behind Albert and Rex.

Albert pushed on, finding a hallway and turning right. Roy appeared by his side, the walking cane held aloft – high and ready to whack down on a skull if one came within range.

"Beverly can be such a worrier," he hissed from the side of his mouth.

Albert wasn't going to, but didn't get the chance anyway because a head poked around the corner.

Roy yelled, "There's the bounder!"

Rex barked and lunged.

Albert cursed loudly because any chance of a surprise ambush was lost, and he let Rex go.

The face was that of a man – Tanya's partner, Albert assumed, for it was there for only a split second. One look at the two men and the dog coming down the hallway was all he needed. The man's head had the same dark hair Albert expected to see, but there was something that instantly troubled Albert.

Something was wrong and Albert knew what it was. Nathan's instant decision to run away was precisely the opposite to what Albert expected. Albert expected a weapon to appear in the man's hand, but he ran and that meant …

"It's a trap!" Albert blurted the words and started running. His head filled with images of the two criminals seeing Rex as the one they needed to defeat and setting a trap for him. Any second now Albert expected to hear his dog yelp in pain.

So it came as a great surprise when the next thing he heard was a man squealing in terror and using words that would make a lumberjack blush.

Rex barked again, and somewhere ahead of Albert a door slammed open.

His knees and hips protested, but now that he was moving, Albert wasn't about to slow his run.

Roy was at his shoulder. "I say. It sounds as though Rex has cornered one of them."

An ear-splitting squeal of pain confirmed it.

The sound of Beverly and Camilla calling their names and asking to know what was happening followed them through the house. Albert let Roy shout an answer – his focus was on finding where Rex had gone.

Passing a door, he saw it was the kitchen and spotted the open door leading outside. Already passing the entrance, he had to hit the brakes hard and grab the doorframe.

Roy clattered into him, almost hitting Albert on the head with his walking cane.

"What do you carry that thing for, anyway?" Albert grumbled in an annoyed manner. "You never use it to walk."

Untangling their limbs, both men reversed direction.

Roy totted the cane smartly, parrying away an imagined sword stroke before chasing after Albert again. Albert was heading out the kitchen door, but he heard Roy's response.

"One never knows when a chap might need a weapon."

There was still no sign of Tanya and that worried Albert. She could so easily be waiting to ambush him or could even be grabbing Camilla now that Rex wasn't there to protect her. He felt a little sick with worry, not least because of what a hardened criminal might do to Beverly since she was just collateral.

However, as he burst into the garden and saw Rex and his latest victim, the worry he felt melted away.

21

BACK AT THE START

Hanging from the limb of a tree was a man in his late twenties. It wasn't Tanya's partner at all, but someone Albert had never seen before. Circling beneath him was Rex, staring upward at the human he'd treed and barking incessantly.

Before Albert could command him not to, Rex launched off the ground with his back legs, leaping as high as he could get only to snap his teeth in thin air as the man hugged the branch again.

"Rex. Enough." Albert's words drew Rex's attention, the dog looking around for his human when his paws touched back down to the ground.

"That was fun," he barked at Albert. "I don't think he can hang on for much longer though, so the really good stuff will begin in a minute." Not wanting to take his eye off the human in the tree for more than a few seconds, Rex delivered his remark and went back to staring at the man's derriere.

Hanging from Rex's lower right canine tooth was a strip of material the same shade as the man's trousers and where the world could now see his underwear, the skin beneath also poked through.

Having heard a man's voice, the man in the tree twisted around to see who was there. He did so carefully, unwilling to take his eyes off the dog for very long.

"Is this your dog?" he asked Albert and Roy, snapping his eyes back down to check on Rex before looking up once more to see how the two old men might answer.

Albert didn't provide an answer. Instead, he whistled and said, "Rex. Here boy."

Rex swung his head around in time to see his human tap his thigh.

"Awww. He's going to fall out of the tree soon. Can't I have a few more minutes of play time?"

"Rex. Here." Albert insisted.

Behind Albert and Roy, Beverly and Camilla burst from the house, both sucking in shocked breaths at the sight they found outside.

"You got him then," Beverly clapped her hands together.

Camilla, however, twisted her head so it was on sideways and then bent at the waist to get an even better look.

"Rupert!"

"Heyyyyy, Camilla," the man in the tree attempted to sound casual about his predicament.

Rex barked at him, and Rupert hugged the branch again. Or, at least, he tried to. His grip, tentative at best, had been losing its effectiveness ever since he first grabbed the branch and swung himself out of the dog's path.

Flicking his gaze between Albert and the man above his head, Rex chose to ignore the command to come to heel. Instead, he took a step back as gravity won its battle and watched with delight as squealing in fright the man fell to the ground.

Rex curled his lips, snarling audibly and visibly as the man covered his face with his arms and tried to curl into a protective ball.

Albert arrived at Rex's side, picking up his lead and ruffling the fur between his ears.

"Well done, Rex."

"Well done!" raged the man on the ground, his voice a little muffled by his arms as they encircled his face. "Well done? He bit me! I'm bleeding!"

Albert cocked an eyebrow. "I should say you probably had it coming."

Rex wagged his tail, but gave the man on the ground another growl when he dared to risk a peek in Albert's direction.

"You can get up now," Albert advised, tugging at Rex's lead and backing up a few paces. The man peered through his fingers, gauging whether it was truly safe to do so or if the dog was going to maul him.

Rex curled his lips again, enjoying the effect the simple expression of potential threat had.

Albert twisted around to look back at Camilla, only to find she was arriving at his side. She didn't stop there though, she went right past him and up to the man on the ground, standing over him with her fists on her hips.

"Rupert Grainger, you get off the ground and explain yourself right now!"

Rupert risked another glance at the dog, who showed his teeth once more. Rex's heart was no longer in it though. He'd had his fun and quite fancied a lie down now, truth be told.

Albert gave the lead a tug, taking Rex back another yard.

The unmistakable sound of a siren pierced the country air. It was more than a mile away, Albert judged, but had to be for them.

"So much for the stealthy approach," he muttered. He was feeling grumpy and didn't bother to listen much to what followed as the man with the ripped trousers slowly got to his feet and stood up.

Rupert Grainger was a former suitor of Camilla's and one who chose to reject her rejection as unacceptable because he was clearly the right one for her in his opinion. He was who she'd seen lurking in the shadows. It was Rupert stalking her, not the Gastrothief's agents.

It put Albert right back to where he'd been: nowhere.

With the raging siren getting ever louder, Albert left Roy and Beverly to keep an eye on Camilla while she yelled at Rupert – just to be sure she didn't hit him with anything, and he took Rex around the house to meet the police at the front door.

He already knew the next hour or two would be lost as he attempted to explain his outlandish claims. There was no way around it – he'd been certain Camilla was being targeted by the Gastrothief's people and let his overconfidence take control of his mouth.

Now he was going to have to suffer the indignity of being lectured on the damage of wasting police time. They wouldn't charge him, but his children might catch wind, and it would embarrass them in turn.

Albert wanted something to kick.

The cops were still a couple of minutes out, so for thoroughness – it was becoming his watchword – Albert took out the list of wine experts and his phone. If it wasn't Camilla being targeted, which seemed highly unlikely now, it had to be one of the others.

Who though? With one on holiday in Scotland and one retired and well into his eighties, it only left two. Leon Harold and Andrew Baker-Brown. Albert had spoken with Andrew Baker-Brown just a few short hours ago, but called him again – just to be thorough.

He got the same answer as before – that Andrew had not seen anyone hanging around and had no reason to believe he might be targeted by anyone. The difference between now and this morning was Andrew's tone. During their first call, he had been indulgent and though he made it clear that he wanted to get off the phone and get on with things, he was nevertheless, polite.

Now he was less so and ended the call by requesting that Albert not call him again. He hung up before Albert could respond.

His call to Leon Harold went to Becky who was still manning the reception desk at First Press Wines. That he didn't have a mobile number for Leon was irksome, and Becky refused to give it to him. Leon Harold had left the premises anyway and was on his way to the awards ceremony in the castle grounds of Royal Tonbridge Wells.

Albert's second call ended just as the police car swung into the top end of the driveway. He pocketed his phone, muttering unhappily about the trials of the righteous man.

The first car to arrive contained a pair of male constables. Constables Entwistle and Greaves were young and hoping for action as the first on the scene. Their disappointment when Albert explained the truth was apparent.

While Greaves remained with the car to radio in the update – there were other cars en route – Albert took Constable Entwistle around the house to find Camilla.

They were no longer outside the kitchen in the shade of the tree, but had moved inside where it was warmer. Albert knocked on the back door before letting himself in, Rex leading and the constable following.

Constable Greaves, the one left by the car, radioed his partner to be let in. To Albert's surprise and great relief, the other squad cars speeding in their direction had all been turned around and the constables at the scene had little interest in his false claim about the Porker factory arsonists.

Indeed, when they quizzed him on the subject, it seemed they were only doing so to clarify a point of confusion.

Side-lined while the cops worked, Albert's eyes fell upon a familiar-looking magazine. He picked it up. It was this month's copy of Wine and Country with Leon Harold's beaming smile gracing the cover.

Camilla, standing just a few feet away, sighed audibly.

"I guess I won't get to attend the gala this year," she griped grumpily, her comment aimed at Rupert though she didn't bother to look his way. "Even if I leave now, I'd only get there for the end of it."

"You can't leave just yet, Miss," advised Constable Entwistle.

Camilla frowned in her disappointment. "See?"

Albert asked, "You were receiving an award?"

With a shake of her head, Camilla said, "Oh, no, nothing like that. To win you need to be nominated and because I work freelance, I don't have a sponsor who would benefit from me winning anything. I was going because it's nice to see my peers. Most of them anyway. It's why I am all dressed up." She indicated her outfit. "I don't usually dress like this to hang around the house. Anyway, the awards are all a bit of a game. It's not like winning is a prestigious award given by one's peers. It's not an Oscar."

"Leon Harold seemed very excited to be getting one," Albert remarked, curious to hear how Camilla might respond.

She snorted a small laugh though it was clear she wasn't feeling amused.

"He's been trying to beat Simon Major for years. I don't think Simon cared one way or the other – they are very different men. Getting his face on the cover of Wine and Country is the pinnacle of success in Leon's opinion."

Albert stared down at the cover again, then placed it back on the kitchen counter where he'd found it. The police were getting ready to put Rupert in the back of their car but were to return to take a statement from Camilla.

Roy sidled over to Albert. "I say, old boy, Beverly is getting a mite anxious about the fish. Will we need to stay much longer?"

Albert doubted the fish were in any danger of losing their freshness - it was about the temperature of a refrigerator outside, but he wasn't going to argue when Beverly had so generously driven him about today.

Coughing loudly in that obvious manner one does when attempting to attract attention, Albert smiled at the constables.

"Are we required, gentlemen? We have no business here, so if you are done with us …"

The two young cops exchanged a glance, a silent question passing between them before Greaves said, "No, Sir. Thank you. You can go."

Albert checked with Camilla, making eye contact so she could have the final word. She thanked him for his interest and even apologised for her idiot of an ex-boyfriend.

"I'm sorry for making you worry," Albert returned her apology with one of his own. "It would seem I had this wrong from the start."

The attractive young wine connoisseur crossed the room to place a hand on Albert's arm.

"You took an interest and were trying to help, Albert. Don't be too hard on yourself. Besides, I'm glad you were here." She shifted her gaze downward to meet Rex's eyes and gripped his head with both hands, ruffling and scratching his ears. "And you, Rex, you big hero, you."

Rex wagged his tail enthusiastically and nudged Camilla's hands when she stopped fussing him – heroes require plenty of affection.

"He bit me," complained Rupert as the cops led him across the kitchen on their way to the front door. "I need stitches in my bum."

Camilla snapped her reply without bothering to look Rupert's way, "You deserved to get bitten."

He lapsed into something close to silence, muttering under his breath about dogs and cops and women.

To finish things off, Albert stuck out his hand for Camilla to shake.

"Good luck with your career in wine."

His remark caused a contented smile and a shrug.

"Thank you, Albert. If only my taste in men was as refined."

Rupert rolled his eyes, but got ignored by everyone.

Camilla walked them out as any decent host might, shaking hands once again before they could leave. Beverly did nothing to hide her desire to get moving, making several comments about the nice fish supper she had planned and about how the sun was already dipping toward the horizon.

However, no sooner were they in the car and heading home, than Albert's phone rang, and the plan changed yet again.

22

WHAT REX KNOWS

"It's where?" Beverly wanted Albert to repeat what he had just said, but it was her husband who answered.

"Marston, darling. It used to be a Royal Airforce base, don't you remember? Now it's a commercial airport. They fly to Europe mostly, I believe. Their runway is not long enough for the larger aircraft that might cross the Atlantic. They have a few private clubs that fly out of there too. Old Digger Muldoon has a plane there."

Beverly frowned at Roy. "What are you wittering on about, you daft old fool? RAF Marston? I've never heard of it. Are you sure the pair of you aren't making it up?"

The question came due to the request that she make yet another pitstop on her way home. She wanted to get her fish into a marinade of garlic, herbs, and olive oil – she'd been telling the occupants of the car all about it for the last ten minutes. The men knew she was using the fish as an excuse to curtail any further investigation on their part. Not that either was brave enough to state their belief out loud.

Following Albert's phone call, however, they wanted her to stop in at an airfield.

"It's right on the way home, love," Roy had explained. "We have to drive right past it." This wasn't entirely true, but the detour to get there was only a very small one.

The call came from Albert's eldest son, Gary, who much to his own surprise had found the car the Gastrothief's agents parked at Alice and Glen's B&B. They had taken it to Marston Airport where the carpark was fitted with number plate recognition software for ticketing purposes.

Albert couldn't know it, but Tanya and Baldwin always used long term carparks to dump cars. Vehicles were there for months sometimes and in the vastness of a giant parking lot a single car could get ignored indefinitely. That most now have number plate recognition bothered them not one little bit as they never planned to return to pay the ticket. The car could sit there forever for all they cared.

Beverly did not wish to stop off at Marston airport to look at a car and her thoughts on the matter did not need to be expressed. However, Albert could see her resistance waning.

"It could be really important ..." he intoned his voice with the amount of gravity he felt the situation required and it did the trick.

"Oh, all right," Beverly sagged.

As with everything, going to see the car could prove to be another pointless expedition. The police were the better people for the task, but after the drama at Camilla's house, Albert wasn't about to make another call. Besides, what would he even tell them?

Tanya – Albert had trained himself to think of her by the name he thought might actually be hers since he knew Suzie was fake – and her partner were not yet tied to any crime. Albert knew he would sound like a raving lunatic if he tried to explain why he wanted the local police to look at their car.

His own children, who would use their authority to access the car if he asked them to, were all at work in London. Not only was the car and everything to do with it, not in their area so they couldn't command local officers to act on their behalf, they also couldn't get to it themselves.

It was going to be Albert or no one and he knew it.

At the entrance to the long-term carpark, Albert insisted he would pay for the ticket on the way out. Their time inside would be measured in minutes, of course, not hours or days, but even so, Albert suspected it would cost him more than a nice lunch out. Airport carparks are like that.

Once they were inside, the unenviable task of finding the car began. They were looking for a black BMW 5 series, and they knew the plate number, but Alice could have been wrong about the colour and the make and the model – Albert's experience had taught him people rarely get it right. So they went slow and checked all the cars that were dark colours, and German makes, or a biggish car that a person might confuse with a BMW 5 series.

As it transpired, Alice knew her cars and they found it in under ten minutes.

Clearly relieved that they wouldn't have to search the whole carpark, Beverly asked, "What now?"

Rex was sitting up on the backseat. He didn't know where they were, but there were no food smells to be had, so he wasn't all that interested. The humans were talking about something, and he listened briefly to pick out any key words that might suggest they were stopping for food or that there might be something else going on. He got nothing though and was about to lie back down when his human announced his intention to get out.

Exercise was always better than being in the car.

Wagging his tail, Rex nudged at the door when his human grabbed the door handle, and bounded out onto the tarmac the second the door was open far enough for him to shove his head through.

"Stay close, Rex," Albert commanded, not bothering to clip him onto the lead. There were no other cars around and no sign of anyone performing any kind of security check. This was good because he expected to set off the car's alarm.

It was also good because Rex chose that precise moment to go completely nuts.

Inside Beverly's car the smells outside had been masked, and though it was faint now, there was no denying that he could detect the odour of a substance he had been taught to recognise. At the police dog academy, Rex loved the training and the games they played. He enjoyed it even though he felt his human handlers made it too easy. He'd kept quiet when he caught a faint, but undeniable whiff of it at the bed and breakfast. There had been nothing to show his human then. That was no longer the case.

Right now, his nostrils were filled with a scent he knew he was supposed to react to, and he was alerting his human in the only way he knew how – he was barking loudly and incessantly at the black BMW.

"Goodness, what's got into him?" asked Beverly, her shocked face staring at Rex through the driver's window.

Albert was about to ask Rex the same thing, but the words froze in his mouth. He knew what Rex was doing – he was alerting. Albert hadn't worked with police dogs directly during his decades of service, but the dogs and their handlers were always around. The behaviour he could see Rex displaying was one he'd seen other dogs perform. Not only that, he'd seen Rex do it before too.

Crouching to get his arms around the dog's chest, he stroked Rex's head and calmed him.

"Good boy, Rex. Well done. You can smell something, can't you, boy?"

Albert got a lick on his chin for that one as Rex proudly told Albert what a clever good human he was.

Too curious to stay in the car, Roy got out to 'give Albert a hand' a comment that got him a tired mumble and a dismissive wave from his wife.

"Need me to keep a lookout, old boy?" Roy asked as he looked around to see if there was anyone in sight. Rex had made so much noise that anyone within a half mile had to have heard him. Mercifully, there was no sign of anyone coming.

He got a nod from Albert, who rapped his knuckles politely on Beverly's window. When she powered the glass down a few inches, he asked, "Your spare tyre is in the boot, yes?" He already knew where it was on this model of car – the question had been nothing more than an opening line to get Beverly to operate the boot catch.

Confused about what he wanted and being sure to remind Albert to be careful with her bag of fish, she pressed the button and the boot lid opened.

Carefully handing the fish to Roy, Albert lifted the boot liner and fished around for what he needed. Withdrawing from the boot with the hub spanner in his right hand, Albert hefted the piece of iron and advanced on the BMW. He hadn't tossed a car in decades, and when last he did, they were far simpler things to get into and explore. Modern cars were filled with all manner of hidden recesses, but Albert didn't expect to need to go that deep.

The Gastrothief's agents were not expecting anyone to look through the car, and would have aimed to take everything with them when they abandoned it, probably wiping it down thoroughly to remove any prints.

Albert would get Gary to quietly arrange for the car to be towed and thoroughly examined later. Right now, he was going to smash a window and hope Tanya and her partner had been in enough of a flustered hurry to have left something behind.

Raising the spanner in his right hand he aimed it squarely at the centre of the driver's side window and shielded his face using his left arm. Just as he was about to swing the tool, he stopped.

The keys were in the ignition.

Lowering his left hand, he tried the door handle and snorted a laugh when it opened.

They hadn't bothered to lock it. They just parked it, emptied it, and walked away.

"It's not locked?" asked Roy, abandoning his task as lookout when he heard his neighbour open the car door.

Roy's voice acted as a prompt to get Albert moving.

"Take that side, Roy," he pointed to the passenger side. "Check the glovebox and under the seat. In fact, look anywhere you can think of to look."

Hustling around to the other side of the car, Roy asked, "What am I looking for?"

"Anything that isn't part of the car."

Roy opened the front passenger door and climbed inside, rooting around with his fingers and emptying the glovebox.

Albert sank to his knees, resting them on the damp tarmac as he placed his head on the carpet to look under the driver's seat. He couldn't see anything and rooting around with a hand confirmed there was nothing to find. The door bins were spotless, so too the pocket in the back of the front seats.

Rex got impatient and barked again.

The suddenness of the noise spooked Albert, making him jump. Jerking his head, he whacked it against the underside of the steering wheel and then on the plastic bit on the front of the driver seat when he automatically jolted away from the first blow.

Rubbing his forehead and the back of his skull, he extricated himself from the driver's footwell to see what Rex wanted.

"It's in the boot!" barked Rex at a lesser volume. "I get that you can't smell it, that's why I am standing here pointing at it with my head. I don't want to call you dumb … but, come on."

Nodding to himself – he should have asked Rex where to look – Albert used the car to lever himself back to upright and joined Rex.

The boot lid opened with a press of a button and swung upward to reveal the interior space.

Rex hopped up to place his front paws on the lip and looked inside.

It was completely empty.

Roy joined them, all three sets of eyes staring into the dark and empty space.

"There's nothing in there, old boy," Roy remarked, stating the obvious, but also missing the point which Albert then tried to explain.

"Police dogs are trained to signal an alert when they smell certain things. The three scents they are most commonly taught are cash, drugs, and explosives." Albert fell silent, giving himself a moment to think. Rex couldn't tell him which it was and doubted the dog would understand the difference. He didn't need Rex to tell him though, he already had a pretty good idea. "I think there were explosives in the car."

Roy's eyes flared. "Golly."

"What's that?" Albert asked, spotting something in Roy's right hand.

As if only then remembering that he was holding it, Roy lifted his arm.

"Oh, well, ah, it's the only thing I found that wasn't part of the car. It's just a scrap of paper though. It looks like it might be off the cover of a magazine or something. Sorry, I thought it might be a clue for a moment. Silly really. You said to look for anything …"

Albert's brain ground to a halt, focusing everything on a single thought, a single memory. Roy was still talking, but his words passed by Albert's ears without making it into his head.

When Roy finally realised Albert wasn't listening, he stopped talking, but worried about his friend's vacant expression, chose to wave a hand in front of his eyes.

"Everything all right, old boy?"

Albert bit his bottom lip. He was aware of Roy, but his brain was going at triple speed, joining imaginary dots as he checked whether he might have just seen the answer.

"I need to go back to the bed and breakfast. There's something I have to check on," he murmured the announcement, speaking to Roy, but talking more to himself. "And I need to make another phone call."

"Back to Whitstable?" Roy questioned with a glance at his wife, sitting impatiently waiting in the driver's seat of their car. "The old girl won't like that."

Albert murmured, "No choice." Then with a twitch he broke the spell and came back to the present. Speaking with renewed vigour, he remarked, "I can take a cab. No need to put yourself out any further."

"Nonsense, old boy. In it together to the end. That's how we did it in the RAF."

Albert lifted his hands to grip the BMW's boot lid. He was going to close it, but as he did the first rays of moonlight caught on something in the far left corner of the car's boot and he froze once more.

Letting the boot lid rise once more, he leaned in to get it. The object, trapped by the removeable floor of the boot, wouldn't come, and he had to lift out the panel to release it.

Knowing what it was even before he picked it up and wishing he was wrong, nevertheless, Albert held the shiny thin object in the air for Roy to see.

23

A TROUBLING FIND

"What is that?" asked Roy.

Albert blew out a tired breath of resignation before saying, "It's a detonator cap." All question that Rex might have been barking because the boot had once been filled with sausages and now stunk of them was removed. Miming with his hands, Albert explained, "You press this end into the plastic explosive and connect the wire to a circuit. Something like that anyway. When an electric pulse is sent through the wire, the detonator cap goes off and boom, you get a big explosion."

Roy was suitably startled by the revelation. Of course, the find spawned questions.

"Surely though, if we have the detonator cap, they can't set off the explosives," Roy pointed out hopefully.

Beverly powered down her window again. "Are you two planning to take all night?" The window went back up before either man could answer.

Choosing to respond to Roy's comment, Albert said, "They would have a bunch of these. Missing one won't make any difference."

"Oh," said Roy, sounding a little crestfallen. "So what now then?"

Albert took his phone from the inside pocket of his jacket. "Now we make some phone calls." He dabbed the screen with his right index finger. Dabbed it again. Then swore loudly, tipping his head back and cursing to the heavens.

Roy guessed, "Battery flat?"

Albert hung his head. "All the numbers are in it," he all but wailed. "I don't know any of them off the top of my head."

"Who do you need to call?"

Albert gritted his teeth, compiling a short list. "One of my children; probably Gary. The Gastrothief's agents are planning to blow something up and that means we need the anti-terror squad. Also, I believe they are going to target Leon Harold. It's the magazine thing – he was on the cover and … well, I need to go back to the bed and breakfast they were staying in to check something."

Beverly's window powered down again, her expression dark and moody now.

"Roy Hope," she narrowed her eyes at her husband. "A word if you please."

Roy and Albert swung their heads in her direction, neither feeling particularly excited at the prospect of breaking their news.

Albert nodded his head at Roy and took a step forward. When Roy matched him, Albert quickly reversed his step and slunk around the side of the black BMW with a criminal grin on his face.

Left to face the music alone, Roy found himself wilting under his wife's gaze.

"Kitten," he started.

The wagging finger appeared before he could get the second word out.

"Don't you try to sweet talk me, Roy Hope," Beverly growled. "You've got some daft plan up your sleeve, haven't you? What is it now?"

"We need to go back to Whitstable, love. There's something Albert has to check."

Beverly would have spat out her false teeth if she had any.

"You want to do what! I'm going home, Wing Commander Hope and you had jolly well better decide that you are coming with me."

It wasn't often that Roy and Beverly ever came to disagree about anything. Their marriage had been a joy from the day they tied the knot, but even though Roy liked to keep the status quo exactly where it was, there were times when he knew he had to disappoint his bride.

Right now was one of those times.

Opening her car door, he crouched and took her right hand, holding it to his face as he caressed it.

"My darling, I love you more than anyone or anything in this world, but I need to help a friend tonight. I must do this because that is who I am. That is the man you married, and were I to change, I would no longer be worthy of your love."

His words and the tone in which he employed them had the effect he knew they would: Beverly folded.

"Oh, Roy. You're going to do something dangerous. I can tell. Promise me you won't get hurt. I can't … I don't want to go on without you."

Roy lifted his right hand to caress her face and leaned in to kiss her tenderly on the lips.

"Grill me some bacon, darling. I'll be back for breakfast."

Beverly's almost tearful eyes narrowed once again, and she aimed a swipe at Roy's head as he swiftly ducked back out of the car.

"You're a rogue, Roy Hope," she yelled through the open door. "I'm not coming to get you if you end up in jail, you know."

Albert did his best to hide his sniggering, but his shoulders were shaking too much.

"Grill me some bacon," he repeated, laughing his way around the words. "That's a good one."

Beverly started her car and gunned the engine. Albert snagged his bag and suitcase from the backseat just before she set off, and the two friends got a last sorrowful shake of her head as Beverly turned the car around and drove it back toward the carpark's exit.

"I guess we need a cab then," said Roy, patting his pockets to make sure he had his wallet.

Albert lifted the black BMW's keys into the air and jingled them.

24

GET THE BOMB SQUAD!

A lbert had voluntarily given up driving many years earlier – his eyesight and his reactions just weren't up to it. But he still had his driver's licence and considered that this was one of those occasions when needs must.

Rex got into the back of the car, stretching out across the bench seat as Roy settled into the front. In the driving seat, Albert gave himself a few seconds to become familiar with the controls – operating the wipers and the indicators and making sure the headlights came on. When he accepted that to delay any longer was just putting the task off, he selected reverse, thanked his stars the car was an automatic – one less thing to have to think about – and reversed out of the parking spot.

At the exit barrier, his debit card took care of the bill, which wasn't as horrendous as he expected, and they were off.

It was a stolen car – he'd stolen it - which came with a few concerns, but Albert wasn't going to let that worry him or slow him down. Not being able to alert Gary to the explosives was a blow, but he would be able to ask Alice to charge his phone when he got to the B&B. He only needed enough juice to make a couple of phone calls after all.

They were only a few minutes outside of Whitstable, and on a darkened country road devoid of other traffic. To Albert's mind all he needed to do was get to Whitstable. It was a short drive on an empty road which was why he was prepared to do it.

Five minutes into the journey, the lights of Whitstable were beginning to appear and there were streetlights illuminating the road. Albert had relaxed, his hunched posture and nervousness about driving diminishing with each mile.

Then he caught sight of the flashing lights in his rear-view mirror.

Sensing Albert tense, Roy asked, "Everything okay?"

Albert flicked his eyes to the mirror again, this time counting not one but three cars with their roof lights strobing through the trees to his rear.

A heartbeat later, the lead car shot into sight, cresting a small rise to enshroud the liberated black BMW with its headlights.

Sucking some air through his teeth, Albert admitted, "We may be in a spot of bother."

Roy caught sight of the flashing strobe lights too, twisting in his seat for a better look.

Albert slowed his car, making sure he was well below the speed limit; not that he thought it would make much difference to a judge.

However, the lead police car made no attempt to slow down as it approached the rear of Albert's car and swept around him doing double the posted fifty miles per hour.

The next two squad cars did likewise, all three racing to get somewhere.

Watching them accelerate toward Whitstable, Albert murmured, "I've got a bad feeling about this."

Roy said nothing, both men watching the blazing red taillights dwindle into the distance until with a huff of decision, Albert pressed the BMW's accelerator into the floor. The car bucked instantly, the powerful German three litre engine responding with a crisp, throaty exhaust note.

Pressed back into their seats, two men and a dog all stared through the front windshield as Albert kept pace with the squad cars. He made no attempt to catch them, keeping the rear car in sight as they arrived back among the houses of the seaside resort, and all were made to slow their pace.

It was soon obvious the police were heading for the seafront, and before they got there, Albert and Roy saw their destination.

Close to the harbour, yet more flashing strobe lights illuminated the buildings in an unmistakable manner. There were dozens of police at the scene – whatever it was.

When the cars he was following angled into the kerb and parked, Albert cruised on past them, glancing their way when he felt able to risk taking his eyes off the road. He counted six squad cars and a fat handful of officers in uniform. The cops he chased all the way to the town were getting out of their cars, moving swiftly to join the action.

The building they were parked in front of had the words 'Whitstable Oyster Hatchery' painted in three-foot-high letters on the front façade. Now Albert knew what he was looking at and he cursed yet again.

"They've hit the oyster hatchery," he growled the words through his clenched teeth. Yet again, he was a step behind and too slow on the draw.

Or was he? The building looked intact, and with that acknowledgment, Albert's pulse went through the roof.

He stomped on the brake, shooting Rex off the back seat with an annoyed 'woof' of shock. Roy found himself catapulted forward, held in check only by his seatbelt, but Albert didn't have time for apologies or explanations.

The car to his rear gave a blast of horn, drawing the eyes of over half the police milling about in front of the hatchery as Albert cranked his steering wheel hard to the left and mounted the kerb.

The car protested, a hard thump radiating through the chassis as it ground out on the lip of the pavement with a small shower of sparks. Albert didn't care – it wasn't like it was his car.

"We're getting out?" guessed Roy, reaching for his seatbelt, but checking Albert's plan first.

A constable was already heading in their direction, sent by a superior to move the idiot in the black BMW along. That was fine by Albert; he needed their attention.

Ripping his own seatbelt off, Albert called for Rex to follow him, and let Roy know, "That place is going to explode! And it's full of police!"

Bailing out of the car with Rex right on his tail, Albert raised both hands to draw attention his way and dashed around the car.

"Get back in your car and move along, Sir," the constable commanded, raising his hands to his sides to form a barrier with which he meant to push Albert back.

"Where's your boss?" Albert demanded in response. In his hand he held the detonator cap "Who's on-scene commander? Dammit man everyone here is in danger!" Albert barked his questions in a manner that trucked no argument.

A sergeant, the one who had sent the young constable to see Albert off, asked, "Who are you? What danger?"

Now that the constable was unsure what was expected of him, his arms began to fall and Albert nimbly sidestepped him, Roy following close behind.

Rex had his nose in the air, sniffing to detect the explosives again. His human was smarter than he often gave him credit for, Rex acknowledged. He understood what had been in the boot of the car and was acting.

However, Rex couldn't smell the explosives now. Was it just that he was upwind and couldn't catch it? He set off to explore only to find Albert grabbed his collar and held him in place before he could.

"Listen," Albert begged the sergeant. "You've got to get everyone out of that building right now." Seeing the doubt of the faces looking back at him – more officers were turning around to listen with every second – and the utter lack of response, he tried to explain at speed. "The hatchery has been robbed, right? And there are people who work there missing, yes?"

The sergeant who first addressed him scrunched his face. "How could you …"

Albert cut right over the top of him. "The people who did this are the same ones who hit the Porker factory in Reculver yesterday. They set fire to that to cover their tracks, or … look I don't know why they did it, but that black BMW is their car and my dog," Albert swung a hand to indicate Rex, "is a former police dog. He alerted when we found the car. And then I found this in the boot." Albert let go of Rex's collar to grab the sergeant's hand and slapped the detonator cap into it.

When half a dozen cops peered into the sergeant's hand and two seconds passed without anyone doing anything, Albert blew his top.

"Do something, man!"

The old man's bellow of disbelieving rage finally shocked a reaction from the dumbfounded police officers. Old men screaming about explosives was not what they had expected. This looked like nothing more than a robbery. A slightly unusual robbery – I mean, who steals oyster hatchlings? Nevertheless, the crazy old guy with the dog knew all about what was going on somehow, he was in their faces, and he *was* holding a detonator cap. They could quiz him about it later. In the meantime, the only prudent thing to do was evacuate the building.

Shouting ensued, the oyster hatchery spewing uniformed officers and a pair of men in suits back onto the darkened pavement in a flurry of motion. Faced with a possible bomb, the cops retreated a safe distance, setting up barriers and closing the road all within just a couple of minutes.

The Bomb Squad were summoned, though it would take them half an hour to get to the site, and once all those things were done, silence fell.

Albert, Roy, and Rex were swept up into the evacuation, taken with the police officers as they moved back to a perceived safe distance a hundred yards away. More officers were coming, and a mobile command unit, while those officers already at the hatchery were deployed to go door to door, evacuating families from their homes and from two restaurants at the nearest end of the town's centre where they were deemed to be too close to the potential epicentre of the blast.

"How much explosive are we talking about?" asked Sergeant Norton. He'd introduced himself and made sure to learn the names of the two men now effectively if not actually in his custody.

Albert did his best to explain. "I have no idea. The dog alerted when we got to the car."

"Which you say belongs to the people who set the fire at the Porker factory yesterday?"

"Yes."

"How do you know that?"

Sergeant Norton was thinking in calm, logical terms now that the panic of getting people clear of the hatchery was complete. His questions were precisely the right ones to ask, but Albert had no answers to give. Or rather he did, but they were not ones that would do him any favours. Regardless, Sergeant Norton was waiting for an answer.

Albert needed to tell him something and couldn't think of a way to get around the longwinded tale of the Gastrothief.

Salvation, of a sort, came in the unexpected form of a new arrival.

"What is going on? demanded Chief Inspector Quinn. "Sergeant Norton, report."

Albert tried to speak, but got an insistent index finger held in the air to stop him while Chief Inspector Quinn stared at Sergeant Norton, waiting for his answer.

Roy frowned. "I say, that's a tad rude."

Quinn ignored him too, never so much as giving an indication he'd heard the comment while Sergeant Norton floundered and struggled to makes sense of the last ten minutes.

When he'd heard enough, Chief Inspector Quinn summed up.

"So two old men arrive in what they confess to be a stolen car and then distract the entire police operation with a story about explosives. What's next, Norton? The dog is going to deactivate the bomb?"

Unable to stay quiet, Albert said, "Are you quite mad? Are you going to send people in there and risk their lives? What if I am right?"

Quinn aimed a disparaging sneer in Albert's direction.

"Now that you have created all this havoc, I am forced to treat the situation as I find it. Taxpayers' money will be spent at an alarming rate while the bomb squad and dozens of Kent police all scurry around trying to keep everyone safe from a danger that I fully expect to have never existed. That's not to mention all the displaced families and the local businesses who are losing money because of this little 'stunt'. You alerted my officers to the location of the *supposed* Reculver arsonists only a few hours ago, did you not?"

Sergeant Norton hadn't known about that, his face revealing that he now felt foolish for listening to Albert's wild tale of arsonists and bombers.

Albert gritted his teeth. "Indeed I did. Are you sticking with your daft theory that the Porker factory was burned down by the owners?"

Showing his teeth, Quinn leered in Albert's face.

"You, Sir, are a reckless old fool with a careless attitude and a child's imagination." Seeing the anger in Albert's face and liking it, Quinn pressed on. "What? You think I don't know about your three children in the Met? You think I don't know about their daft 'secret' investigation?" he put air quotes around the word 'secret', "The Gastrothief, isn't it?" Quinn chuckled.

Albert felt his cheeks colour, warmth filling them as he silently rode out the public demeaning.

"They are all in for a rough time after this, I can assure you. I already filed a complaint against your daughter. Now there's a woman who got too big for her boots." The chief inspector was now playing to his audience, half a dozen cops listening in and knowing to give an approving smile when their boss made a joke.

Albert felt his right fist clench.

Dismissively, Chief Inspector Quinn turned away, speaking over his shoulder as he left Albert behind.

"See these two are comfortable and don't let them out of your sight. I plan to charge them both with disturbing the peace and whatever else I think will stick once the bomb squad have proven there is no bomb here."

Looking around at the sea of disapproving or even angry faces, Albert wondered if this might be close to what it felt like to be a prisoner of war. They were to be held captive amid an ocean of hostility until such times as the chief inspector saw fit to do something else with them.

He was about as miserable as he could get. Worse yet, his best result involved him being right about the explosives and it was a thing he would not allow himself to wish for.

Placed in the back of a police squad car, in deference to their age and because the car was warm, Roy nudged Albert's shoulder with his own.

"Chin up, old boy. It's always darkest before the dawn. The righteous man rarely gets to walk an easy path."

Albert couldn't think of a reply to give. He knew Roy was right, and he knew that at some point his theory about a master criminal would be proven accurate. His actions would be vindicated when that finally happened, but it was little comfort to him now.

Focusing on Rex, who was sitting between Albert's knees in the back of the squad car with his jaw resting on Albert's left knee, Albert thought about the explosives and what else they might be employed for if not to blow up the oyster hatchery.

When the answer came to him, he almost jumped out of his seat.

25

BIN BAGS, OYSTER BEDS, AND BULLETS

Roy had been contentedly dozing off when he was jolted back to alertness by Albert's sudden exclamation.

"I say, old boy. You could give a chap a little warning."

Albert had his face pressed against the glass of the window, his eyes darting this way and that as he looked to see who was actually watching them. It didn't appear to be anyone.

He tried the door handle, only at that point thinking to question whether they might have been locked in. The door shifted.

Shooting his head and eyes back at Roy, he said, "I've just figured it out." He checked his brain again. "I think," he added with distinctly less conviction. "Rex will be able to tell if I am right or not."

At the sound of his name, Rex lifted his head. He'd also been attempting to go to sleep and had been steadfastly refusing to remove his jaw from Albert's knee while his human was moving around.

"We're going somewhere?" Rex asked.

Albert opened the door just a couple of inches to see what would happen, then peered through the gap and looked around.

There was no chance they could get more than a few yards without being spotted, but biting his lip and questioning what he should do, an opportunity presented itself.

The bomb squad were arriving.

Swiftly swivelling around on the back seat, Albert spat his plan in an urgent torrent of words, "The view to see us is about to be blocked by the bomb disposal truck as it passes. We'll have to be quick, but if we move with it, we should be able to get to the alleyway just across there." Albert pointed to a dark hole between houses fifty yards away.

Roy required no convincing, bracing himself to exit the car right on Albert's tail.

"Ready when you are, old boy."

Albert took a firm grip on Rex's lead and whispered to him, "We're going to need to be quiet, Rex. Do you think you can do that?"

Albert was not expecting an answer though he got one when Rex confirmed his understanding of the plan. The black Bomb Disposal vehicle had just turned into the public carpark where the police had set up their control area and it was slowing down.

He was just about to go when he spotted a radio sitting on the front passenger's seat. He hadn't been able to see it until now, but darting an arm between the seats, he grabbed it and had just enough time to thrust it into a coat pocket.

The bomb disposal van was already alongside them, and with no time to lose, Albert hissed, "Now!" and kicked the back door wide open.

Both men held their breath with nervousness despite jogging as fast as they could to keep pace with the squat black van. It tracked across the carpark heading directly for what clearly the command centre. Albert heard somebody shout to get Chief Inspector Quinn's attention and hugged close to the side of the moving bomb disposal vehicle.

When they drew level with the alleyway, the trio peeled right and hoped for the best - if they were going to be spotted it would happen now.

Three seconds later, the darkness between the buildings swallowed them. No enraged demand for them to stop followed and there came no cries of alarm, not that Albert would have stopped if they had. Running from the police was a new sensation and not one which Albert would claim to enjoy. It was thrilling, but he was out of breath and his nerves felt utterly wrecked.

They kept going, drawn through the alleyway by Rex who was having a wonderful time. Rex didn't know where they were going, but it hardly mattered to him - they were outside and having fun.

With his knees and hips already protesting, and no sign that the police were giving pursuit, Albert chose to slow to walking pace as he reached the end of the alley. The dark passage had taken them from one street to the next, the trio emerging into a quiet road which appeared to be devoid of life.

Where the police had evacuated people from their houses there were no windows lit up from within and where there might usually be cars parked bumper to bumper along the kerb, tonight there were gaps, the residents electing to drive to a hotel or perhaps stay with a relative in another town.

Sucking in air to get their breath back, Albert and Roy did their best to look like two chaps out walking a dog.

"Where are we going?" Roy wanted to know. "You said something about having worked it out?"

Albert spotted another alley on the other side of the street and steered Rex toward it – staying out of sight was the only sensible strategy. They were inside the evacuated zone and the police cordon set up to keep people out and that meant they could move freely to a certain extent.

To answer Roy, he said, "I think it's to do with the tides." They reached a junction in the alley where it met another that crossed it. Albert turned right, heading for the seafront. "Glen – that's the bed and breakfast owner, said that the couple staying there were asking about tide times, and he saw the bloke with a tide book in his hand. The tide was in earlier, which means it must be out now. I don't know why they would want to do it, but if they didn't use the explosives in the hatchery …"

"Maybe they are using it on the oyster beds." Roy finished Albert's sentence.

Albert shrugged his shoulders. "Why else would they want to know about tide times? It's not like they could dig up a worthwhile number of oysters. I was thinking about the whole thing while we were sitting in the back of the police car. For weeks now I have been tracking these weird crimes – chefs, food, and equipment getting stolen from all over the place. Why?"

"Why indeed," agreed Roy.

They reached the mouth of the alley, emerging cautiously to check the coast was clear. They were a hundred yards or more from the harbour and the hatchery now, but the houses were just as evacuated and dark as everywhere else. The seafront was just ahead beyond the final row of houses and stepping out of the alley, Albert realised how close he was now to Alice and Glen's bed and breakfast place.

His feet twitched with indecision, but the detour to grab the rubbish was a short one so he went with it even though it was taking him back toward the police at the harbour.

"I thought we were heading for the beach, old boy?" Roy frowned when his friend went the wrong way.

"We are," Albert assured him, then pointed to the bed and breakfast down the street and explained his need to stop off. "I'm hoping we can just grab the thing I need. If they haven't put any more bags out since this morning, it should be right on top."

Rex looked up. "We're going dumpster diving again?"

Catching his dog's expression, Albert chose to hand Rex's lead to Roy and left them in the street while he snuck into the bed and breakfast's back yard. The lid was down on the rolltop bin, but in what felt like the first piece of good fortune he'd had in days, the black sack containing the bin bags from the guests' rooms was the first one he tried.

He still needed to find the right bin liner inside it, and that took longer than he wanted, but the small bag containing earwax laden cotton buds and Tanya's makeup wipes was there for him to find. The small blue triangle of paper was there too.

Was it what he thought it was? He couldn't be sure, but his confidence was high. Now he really needed to get some charge in his phone. The option of begging Alice and Glen to let him use their electricity was off the table – their place was within the evacuation zone and just as dark and abandoned as everywhere else. Annoyed with himself for letting his phone battery run so low, he resolved to check his theory about the oyster beds. After that, they would get clear of the evacuated part of town and knock on doors until someone was good enough to let him charge his phone.

If he was right, and Albert was sure he was, the Gastrothief's agents had stayed in the area because they still had work to do. He was beginning to get fearful for the size of the operation – clearly it wasn't just Tanya and her accomplice because someone had to transport the people, the enormous amount of wine they stole from the vineyard in Eccles, and now all the oyster hatchlings.

How many might be involved Albert had no idea, but the feeling of being in the dark was becoming a constant companion.

"Got what you needed?" asked Roy when Albert returned with a small, clear plastic bag in his right hand. He got a nod in reply and fell into step as he handed over Rex's lead.

"I need to make some phone calls," Albert remarked, walking quickly to get to the beach. "I still think the people we are after are going to grab Leon Harold. This pretty much proves it," Albert held the plastic bag of trash items aloft.

Roy's eyebrows knitted together. "That looks like a bag full of rubbish, old boy."

"Sorry, yes. I was referring to this." Albert stopped moving to show Roy the small triangle of paper. I think it's the cover of a magazine. The one that had Leon Harold on the cover. This is the rubbish from the room the Gastrothief's agents were staying in. They tried to get Simon Major and failed. He fell to his death and now they are going after Leon Harold instead. We have to stop them, and to do that I need to get my phone working."

"You don't think the police will help?" Roy enquired, his tone laden with the doubt he himself felt.

Albert blew out a hard breath. "You saw how Chief Inspector

Quinn treated me. If I tell him I believe there is about to be a
kidnapping, he will laugh in my face. I can say 'I told you so' when it
happens, but doing so achieves nothing."

Rex's nose, an organ that never stopped working, was snorting in
the air blowing in off the sea. Laden with salt, mud, the distinct
scent of the oyster beds, and …

A scent he knew hit Rex's brain like a firecracker going off.

Albert and Roy had just reached the beach, their near silent
footfalls suddenly audible as their feet crunched onto the gravel.
Albert was still explaining his thinking and was not prepared for his
dog to go berserk.

Rex barked and lunged. They were out there in the darkness
ahead of him. He could smell them and there was no way he was
wrong.

Gripped by panic, Albert reeled Rex in. The dog had given his
arm quite a yank and his shoulder joint was smarting. The bigger
problem was that Rex would be heard by the police and now was
not the time to get caught.

Albert sank to place one knee on the stony ground. "What is it,
Rex?"

"They're here!" Rex barked again despite his human trying to
grab his muzzle to keep him quiet. "They are down there somewhere. You have to let me go! I can catch them!"

"He's barking at something out there on the mudflats," Roy
strained his eyes to see. The moon was hidden behind a bank of
clouds, and though they could see light reflecting off the water
which had receded a quarter mile as the tide ran out, the mudflats
themselves where the oysters could be found, were little more than a
stretch of black.

Albert stared too, both men squinting at the darkness.

Rex barked again and this time he was answered.

By a bullet.

26

HOT PURSUIT

The sound of the shot was followed almost instantly by the zip crack sound of the bullet passing close by their heads. It hit a breaker six yards behind them with another crack of sound.

The sudden unexpectedness of it shocked both Albert and Roy who threw themselves to the pebbles just as another shot was fired.

Roy complained, "I say!"

Rex lunged again, wanting to play his favourite game but also believing the only defence he had for his human right now was to attack.

Albert screamed, "Rex!" as the lead yanked from his hand and his dog shot down the beach toward the mudflats.

A hundred yards away, invisible in a darkness that seemed to absorb the light around it, a woman shouted something.

Albert's head and eyes shot around to look where the sound had come from. It was Tanya he'd heard; he was certain of it.

"Rex!" he bellowed once more, Roy's voice joining his though Albert knew it was fruitless. Rex had left the beach and was splashing through the surface water on his way to the mudflats now. In seconds he would be upon them, and they would shoot him.

Another shot echoed in the dark, the sound of it stealing Albert's next breath. It didn't come their way though, whoever was shooting was aiming at Rex now.

"Baldwin! Come on!"

This time Albert caught what Tanya said and then he saw her. Or it might have been her partner. He couldn't tell, but an indistinct blob of something had splashed through a puddle and illuminated themselves for just a moment.

Swinging his legs around to get them back under his body, Albert snatched the police radio from his pocket. Taking it from the squad car had seemed a prudent move, but at the time he'd thought he might use it to create a distraction so he and Roy could escape the area.

Now he was using it to bring them to him.

He switched it on with a flick of a button and started shouting.

"All units! All units! There are armed assailants on the beach, and they are firing shots toward the town!"

His next words were interrupted by the sound of an engine starting up. Down on the mudflats a set of lights flared into life, the obvious pattern of bright white at one end and burning red at the other stationary for a split second before the vehicle took off like a cat with its tail on fire.

"Who is this?" barked Chief Inspector Quinn, his voice coming over the radio in Albert's left hand. "Identify yourself."

With his eyes tracking the quad bike, for he could tell what it was now that it was moving, Albert lifted the radio to his lips.

"It's Albert Smith, you incompetent fool. Your bombers are on the beach. Get moving."

It was clear that there were already cops moving in his direction, Albert and Roy could hear them shouting and the sound of their boots on the street as they ran. Unwilling to continue his conversation with Chief Inspector Quinn, Albert flicked the radio's power button back to the off position.

The throaty sound of the quad bike racing along the mudflats was punctuated every second or so by the sound of Rex barking.

Another shot rang out, but it must have missed Rex because he barked again before Albert could take his next breath.

Nudging Roy, he said, "Come on, we'd better follow. Rex won't catch them unless they crash that thing, but he might chase it for miles."

Aiming to go down the beach and jog along where it was flat and the wooden breakers ended, he got to take two steps before he heard Tanya shout something else.

He couldn't tell what she said, but figured out the gist of it when his entire world went white.

A series of explosions rippled from one end of the mudflats where they started at the harbour wall and then chased the quad bike and Rex to the north. Each blast shook the ground and sent huge amounts of mud, sand, and oysters into the air.

In the space of a second, twenty explosions obliterated the oyster beds. The resulting shockwave of air hit Roy and Albert like a solid wall. Ripped from their feet, they flew backward to land five yards farther up the beach. Tumbling and crashing, both men managed to avoid serious injury only through the will of God.

Gasping for breath, Albert rolled onto his side to look for Roy.

"Roy," he managed to croak. "Are you alive?"

Roy was on his back, lying still while he conducted a review of the parts of him that hurt. He gave up and came at it from the other direction, trying to figure out what didn't hurt instead.

To reply to Albert's question, he said, "Ow."

It drew a smile and an almost chuckle from Albert – if Roy was able to say something funny, he couldn't be hurt that badly.

Levering himself off the stones, Albert said, "I guess we found the explosives."

Roy put a hand to his mouth. Fingers curled and thumb extended so it looked like a trumpet, he then made a bugle noise before saying, "Hurray," in a droll tone.

Albert gave him a hand up and looked across the desolation that had once been the oyster beds.

Asking a rhetorical question, he said, "Where's Rex?"

27

ONE LAST TASK

R ex was running for his life.

He'd been chasing the quad bike and thought that he might be able to catch it. The mudflats were surprisingly easy to run on. He'd expected to find the surface hard to grip, but it was the opposite. Just under the muddy sand was a layer of hard strata. The humans had seen him coming and panicked, dashing to the quad bike and leaping on it just before he got to them.

Then it had become a test of which could go fastest. There wasn't much in it.

However, when the first explosion rocked the ground beneath Rex's paws, he twisted around in fright to see what had caused the sound and immediately lost his footing. Crashing to the exposed seabed, his momentum caused him to roll and when he popped up again the line of explosions was ripping toward his face.

The game of chase and bite was already lost – the quad bike now too far ahead for him to catch. It was heading inland toward the beach, but Rex was too scared to care about where they were going.

Driven hard by adrenalin, he thrust off with his back legs and ran to get clear before the explosions caught him.

Fifty yards ahead of Rex, Tanya and Baldwin were ripping the stolen quad bike across the beach, aiming at the sea wall. Ten yards shy, Tanya hit the brakes and held on tight, slewing the fat tyres across the pebbles to stop mere inches from the town's high tide defence.

"I told you we should have grabbed him this morning!" snapped Baldwin, climbing off the quad bike while changing the magazine on his Glock 19 handgun. "How did he find us? That's what I want to know. How is it that an old man seems to know where we are going to be?"

Tanya vaulted the seawall. "Stop asking pointless questions, Baldwin. If you weren't such a terrible shot, the dog would be dead, and we would be taking Albert Smith back to the earl tonight."

"We still need to get him. I don't see the dog, but the old men are just over there. We can get him now. Otherwise, he's going to show up in Cornwall. Or the next place. Or the place after that. Get the car, I'll get Albert Smith." He readied his gun, putting one in the chamber and aiming at the two dark forms he could see coming their way. He would shoot whoever the other old bloke was and take Albert at gunpoint. If he even tried to resist, Baldwin would knock him out and carry him.

Tanya grabbed Baldwin's jacket before he could set off. "Don't be so stupid. Can't you see the police?" She pointed to the mass of figures coming from the harbour. Their torches made them easy to identify and Tanya already knew everyone else had been evacuated from the area. It had made stealing the quad bike easy – the police were looking inward at the town, not outward to sea.

Angry that he couldn't do what he felt was necessary, Baldwin shook his jacket free of Tanya's grip.

"What now then? Let him go? The earl won't like that, and Albert Smith is just going to continue interfering."

Tanya pulled the keys to their hire car from her pocket. "What now? We head back to Rochester, get Leon Harold, and get out of here. We need a couple of days to regroup and rest. Then we mount a one-day operation to get Albert Smith. The earl will agree to sanction it and we know where he lives now." She opened the driver's door and paused, talking to Baldwin over the roof. "We come at night, kill the dog, snatch the old man, and no one will ever know we were there. That's how we deal with Albert Smith. What we don't do is panic and get ourselves caught tonight."

Without waiting to hear his response, Tanya slipped into the car and shut her door. The truck with the oyster hatchlings was already on its way back to the earl's lair along with two self-confessed experts from the operation. Finding them had been easy – Tanya watched the hatchery at closing time for two days, picking out two men who went to the pub across the street.

Chatting them up and finding out what they knew had been simple - the fools telling her everything and bragging about how the hatchery couldn't operate without them. She played them off against each other, arranging (in secret) to meet them both when work ended today.

They found her and Baldwin waiting for them with stun guns.

Baldwin slumped huffily into the passenger seat, Tanya barely giving him time to get the door shut before she pulled away.

It was time to get out of Kent, she felt they had already over-stayed their welcome and Albert Smith was enough of a concern that she was looking forward to vacating the area. Did he have a good enough description of them to set the police on their trail? Had he been able to learn anything worthwhile about them?

She didn't think so. He couldn't know their real names and so far as she knew, the strangely intuitive old man was the only one who had any idea what they were up to. How he knew was another question entirely. However, she put that from her head, and thought about the one last task for the day.

She had roughly an hour's drive to get to Rochester where they would find the wine connoisseur the earl believed he needed and there was nothing anyone could do to stop them.

28

ARREST OR REDEMPTION

With the police heading in their direction, Albert decided the beach was no longer a good place to be. They had to move quickly and that was a challenge – their aches and pains were very real and would be far worse in the morning. However, the beach was a long dark strip of land and the police stood little chance of seeing the two shapes sneaking back toward the town.

At the seawall Albert hugged the stone to make himself as hard to see as he could manage and called for Rex. He didn't think his dog had been caught by the explosion – the dog was right on the tail of the quad bike when the blasts occurred, and the quad bike had escaped.

He hadn't seen him since though and was starting to worry. Albert wouldn't leave the area without him even if it did mean the police would catch them again.

Thankfully, having made it to the beach ahead of the oysters, mud, sand, and rock raining back to earth behind him, Rex was looking for his human.

Of course, Rex wasn't looking at all, he was using his nose, and he only needed a few seconds to pinpoint Albert's location.

"He's on his way," Albert whispered to Roy when he spotted Rex coming along the path bordering the beach. The sense of relief he felt was enough that he needed to use the wall for support when his legs went weak.

Rex was safe and didn't appear to be hurt in any way.

He was covered in wet mud though, Albert discovered, when he crouched to give Rex a hug. It was a minor concern he swiftly put to one side.

"Right," he said to Roy, leading him over the seawall. "I've been one step behind ever since I first came across the Gastrothief and it's time to change that. I'm betting everything I've got on one last roll of the dice. They are going to target one of the wine connoisseurs before they leave and blowing up the oyster beds feels like a last act to me."

Roy clapped Albert on the shoulder. "You've been right about everything so far, old boy."

"Not right enough," Albert replied, rejecting the compliment. "I needed to figure out their next moves before they made them, not after. If I had thought to consider what they were doing in Whitstable, I might have looked at potential targets. The oyster hatchery was obvious."

Roy shook his head. "I think you're being a little harsh on yourself there, Albert. But look, you say they are going to target a wine connoisseur and you have a list of their names and numbers."

Albert's jaw dropped open and his slapped his hands to either side of his face.

"I've got a list!" he cried in despair.

Confused, Roy said, "That's what I just said."

Taking his hands from his face, Albert started scrambling through his pockets. He found the piece of paper inside his jacket where it had been all day.

"We could have phoned Leon Harold's place of work at any point in the last few hours," he raged at himself, making a fist with his left hand and whacking himself on the temple. "Arrrrghh! I know they've given me the brush off twice now, but this time I know I'm right. They'll have to listen and get a warning message to him."

Roy caught on. "Ah, yes. I see what you are saying. The battery on your phone needn't have been a barrier at all." Delving into the inside left pocket of his blazer, Roy produced his own phone. "Here, old boy. Use mine."

Albert dialled the number that belonged to the one person he considered to be the most likely target – Leon Harold.

It connected instantly to a voicemail message.

"This is First Press Wines. Our offices are now closed. Please call back between the hours of …" Albert stabbed the red button to end the call and started dialling the next number – that of Camilla Humphries-Bowden.

"I only have Leon's office number," Albert explained as he carefully punched in the digits. "Camilla might have his mobile number, though I doubt it – she didn't make it sound like they were friends, but I'm hoping she can confirm something for me and maybe find me his number."

The phone rang and rang causing Albert to twitch his right foot with impatience. Finally, just when he thought it was going to go to voicemail, it was answered.

"Hello?" Camilla's voice was timid and nervous.

"Camilla, it's Albert, I need your help." His simple sentence cut through everything to deliver only that which was pertinent to the situation.

"Gosh. What do you need?" Camilla was on board instantly.

Albert directed her to find the Wine and Country magazine with Leon Harold on the front cover. She did so, reporting her movements as she rushed through her house to the kitchen. When she had it, Albert asked her to send him a photograph of the bottom right corner. He knew sending photograph messages was a thing a phone could do though the how of it was a bit too much for him.

Two seconds later, the phone in his hand pinged and a small icon appeared.

Looking at the phone when Albert showed him the screen with a what-do-I-do-now expression, Roy said, "I believe you just tap that little thingy in the corner."

Sure enough the icon grew to fill the screen, and there was the edge of the magazine. Albert knew without checking that he was absolutely right, but he took out the bin liner and its content anyway. Taking great care to avoid the earwax coated cotton buds, he pushed the tiny triangle of paper to the surface of the bag and nodded his head.

Where the paper had ripped, it had torn through one of the buttons on the sleeve of Leon Harold's jacket. He hadn't noticed that was what it was on the scrap of paper until now, but it was obvious.

"What's going on?" asked Camilla. "Are you still there, Albert? You've gone very quiet."

"Yes," he replied, unable to take his eyes off the triangle of paper. "The target is Leon Harold. I don't suppose you have a number for him, do you?"

"Gosh, sorry, no," Camilla apologised. "He'll still be at the awards ceremony though. That's only just wrapping up. I have the number for them if you want it."

Feeling like he'd just been hit with a shot of adrenalin, Albert was suddenly alert. Maybe he could still salvage something from this mess. Maybe he was going to be able to lay a trap for them.

"Hold on," he begged, patting at his pockets. "I need a pen." Frantically, he looked at Roy hoping he might have one.

Camilla chuckled. "No need. I can just send it to you as a text message. When you select it, the phone will ask if you want to update your contacts."

"Really?" Albert asked, surprised yet again by the wonders of modern technology.

Another ping heralded the arrival of the phone number he required and effectively ended his call to Camilla.

He thanked her profusely and got off the phone so he could make the next call. This time it was answered immediately.

"Vanessa Parsons."

The voice in his ear was that of a professional young woman – clearly someone involved in the arrangements for the awards event. That she had to know Camilla was his key.

Trying to sound as if he were not in an all-fired hurry, Albert employed brevity.

"Good evening. My name is Albert Smith. I was given your number by Camilla Humphries-Bowden …"

"Oh, Camilla," Vanessa replied in a bubbly manner, cutting Albert off before he could get to his point. "Do you know what happened to her today? All I got was a message saying she couldn't attend."

"So sorry," Albert could talk her ear off if she so desired, but only after he'd made sure Leon Harold was safe and could be kept that way. If Leon was there and would listen, Albert could figure out a way to set a trap. "I need to speak with Leon Harold. It is quite urgent."

Sounding a little put out to be so rudely interrupted, Vanessa nevertheless provided an answer.

"I'm afraid he already left. He didn't even wait for the end of the ceremony. Once he had his award, he made his speech and walked out the door."

Albert felt like punching something. At every turn he was getting defeated.

Refocusing, he asked, "Okay, thanks. Do you know where he went? Would he have gone home? He might be in danger, and I need to speak with him."

Now sounding guarded, Vanessa said, "I'm sorry, I don't have that information. Sorry, I cannot be of any help."

Whether she knew the answers or not, Albert could tell Vanessa wasn't going to give them to him. He thanked her for her time and thumbed the phone's red button to end the call.

Now what?

Albert asked himself the question in the manner of a person who refused to be beaten. There had to be a way to get to Leon Harold.

Clutching at straws, he called Camilla again.

She answered straight away this time. "Albert? Is that you? Did you manage to track down Leon?"

"Camilla, hi. Yes, it's me and no I didn't manage to get him yet.

I know this is a long shot, but do you know anyone who would have his mobile number or any idea where he lives?"

"Gosh. Right, okay. I think I might be able to find someone with his number. You'll have to give me a few minutes to make some calls and put a thing out on social media. I might even find him on there, but whether he replies or not I cannot guess. I can tell you where he lives though."

Albert's heart soared.

"Not his actual address, I'm afraid," Camilla apologised, her words like a pin to the bubble of hope blooming in Albert's chest. "But I do know that he lives right by Rochester airport. He's a flying nut. It's all he ever talks about when he isn't bragging about wine."

Rochester airport. That was something he could use. Hope began to bloom again.

"Camilla if you can get me a number for him, please do. I leave you with that, I need to get the police moving."

Off the phone and with no current need for it, Albert handed it back to Roy and took out the police radio.

He needed to get them to mobilize and protect Leon Harold, but in such a way that they were waiting for the Gastrothief's agents when they came for him. Unable to contact his own children, and knowing the officers under their control were miles away in the capital, he needed the Kent Police.

The instant problem with that was his current standing with the county's law enforcement. He was a worry wart, a troublemaker. He was the boy who cried wolf. Or possibly he was something worse than that and his knowledge of the explosion before it happened might place him in an altogether different category – that of a person of interest.

Given Chief Inspector Quinn's earlier attitude, Albert had to question if he would be taken into custody on sight and held until they could be sure he had no involvement in recent events. He wouldn't blame them for being cautious – people get mightily nervous when things start to explode, but he didn't have the time for it.

Nevertheless, he was an hour from Leon, and he needed help.

The Gastrothief's agents were in Whitstable only minutes ago, and Albert knew they didn't have Leon yet because he had spent the afternoon at the Wine and Country awards ceremony. This was his best chance to make a difference.

But what if they don't try to snatch him tonight?

The tendril of doubt twisted through Albert's gut making him question everything until with a snap, he flicked the radio on and held it to his face.

"Chief Inspector Quinn, this is Albert Smith."

"Where are you Mr Smith? You need to surrender yourself to my officers immediately."

Ignoring Quinn's demand, Albert said, "I was right about the explosives, Chief Inspector, even if I did have the location wrong. I am right about the next thing I am going to tell you too."

"Jolly good. Tell me where you are, and I will gladly listen to whatever you have to say."

A smile creased Albert's face, the first in hours. He didn't believe Quinn for a second. Roy was on the phone to someone – Beverly, Albert assumed. His former Royal Air Force neighbour had retreated a yard and was jabbering in an animated way. Albert let him get on with it.

"The people who set the explosives and just obliterated the oyster beds are now on their way to kidnap a man named Leon Harold. He is a wine connoisseur of some reputation," Albert explained.

Now impatient, Quinn snapped. "Surrender yourself, Mr Smith! I grow tired of your games. How involved in all this are you?"

Albert almost shouted his reply, but conscious that he might be heard – they were only a street away from the beach – he kept his voice calm and steady.

"Leon Harold works for First Press Wines. He received an award today and will be kidnapped by the Gastrothief's agents as a replacement for Simon Major. Simon was their first choice and died attempting to evade capture. You need to send officers to Mr Harold's house so they can be there ready to make arrests. These are the same people who burnt down the Porker factory, raided the oyster hatchery and stole the wine from Chapel Hill Wines. You can solve all three crimes and a whole bunch more with one act."

"I've listened to enough of your nonsense, Mr Smith. The Gastrothief? I've never heard such utter guff. Well, be warned. I am raising a warrant for your arrest. Make things easy on yourself and surrender now."

Albert pursed his lips, puffed out his cheeks, and flicked the radio off.

"We're on our own, old boy?" confirmed Roy. "Good thing I have a plan then."

29

AN UNEXPECTED MODE OF TRANSPORT

"We need the car though," Roy added.

"We can't possibly get there before Tanya and Baldwin," Albert argued with a frown. "They have a huge head start."

"Ah," Roy replied with an air of mysticism. "Like I said, I have a plan."

Not wanting to be the defeatist in the pair, Albert said, "Okay. But I don't think there's any chance we are getting the BMW back, it's right by the oyster hatchery and in full view of the police."

Roy sucked some air through his teeth. "Yes, that is a bit of a pickle. A taxi will do though. We don't need to go far." Roy started walking. "Come on, old boy. I'll explain on the way."

When he had, Albert said, "That is the maddest idea I have ever heard. I could never have come up with it in a million years."

They were heading for the train station where they expected to find a cab, but pushed for time, Albert changed the plan when he spotted an alternative that would suit them even better.

Steering Roy toward it, Albert said, "That will get us there without any hold ups."

Roy was so taken aback his feet actually ground to a halt.

"You're not serious, are you, old boy?"

Albert continued walking, turning around to shrug at his companion.

"We're already wanted men. Stealing a police car won't make things any worse."

The squad car was stationed at the edge of the cordon, blocking the road so that anyone coming into that part of Whitstable wouldn't be able to go any farther. It had probably been abandoned when the mudflats exploded, the cops reacting to the demand to get there by going on foot.

Unfortunately for them, in their haste they left the driver's door open.

Albert opened the back door. "Come along, Rex."

Still coated in mud, Rex jumped onto the bench seat, turned around, and laid himself down.

Roy had never been in a police car prior to today, and after a brief stint sitting in the back of one, he was now going to be the accomplice in stealing another. Beverly was going to kill him if he got caught.

With no good options and Albert already adjusting the driver's seat, Roy accepted his fate and got in.

With their seatbelts on, Albert found the switch for the rooflights and said, "It's been a few years." It was a throwaway line he'd uttered for no good reason other than because it popped into his head. Somehow though, it captured the moment perfectly. They were two men way past the prime of their lives, but there was life in the old dogs yet.

Laughing at their predicament, Albert stomped on the gas and spun the wheel. Though he was tempted to drive like a bat out of hell – they were racing against a pair of kidnappers who had a twenty-minute lead on them – Albert applied some caution.

It probably added two minutes onto their journey, but that was better than crashing because neither his eyesight nor his reactions worked as well as he wanted.

Fifteen minutes after setting off from Whitstable, Albert turned into Marston Airport.

The carpark barrier opened for them just as before, spitting out a ticket and reading the number plate. They already knew there was no camera to record their faces. Had there been, Gary would have been able to identify Tanya and Baldwin hours ago.

Rex had no idea what they were doing back at the airport and was more than a little disappointed there had been no dinner. His human kept a can of dog food and a bowl in his backpack, but that was still in the back of the last car they'd been in.

His human hadn't eaten either which gave Rex some hope that they had come here to get food.

Out of the squad car, Roy led them to a gate, but didn't go through it. It was a seven-foot-high steel turnstile designed to keep people out unless they had a right to go through it. Albert already knew Roy's phone call had not been to his wife, but to an old friend from his RAF days. The chap owned a plane that was parked in Marston, and they were going to use it to get to Rochester. If Leon's house was close to the airport, it was the perfect way to get there ahead of Tanya and Baldwin.

"Here he comes," announced Roy, sounding jubilant. Then in greeting to his friend, he called out, "Digger!"

The man coming their way had to be well into his eighties, but he was sprightly and full of beans.

"Hopeless, you old devil!" Digger Muldoon did something with a card and the barrier was suddenly free to rotate.

The old flyers shook hands and exchanged a few words, but Albert didn't need to say anything about the urgency of their situation – Digger had been fully briefed.

"It's this way," he beckoned, leading them across the tarmac and onto grass. They were heading for a hanger. "You're lucky you caught me here. I was just about to head home. The old girl gets a bit miffed if I stay here too late. Honestly though, she doesn't understand why I come here at all. It's not like I can fly at my age she always says."

Albert jerked. "Who's flying then?" he wanted to know.

Roy raised his right arm, never breaking step as he walked smartly onward.

"Um, you never said you were going to be the one flying, Roy," Albert pointed out.

"Just like riding a bike," Roy remarked. Then before Albert could ask his next question it was answered for him.

He wanted to know what sort of plane they were going to be taking. He'd not thought to question it earlier – the plan was barking mad in the first place, but his imagination had conjured images of small aircraft with half a dozen seats and a couple of engines. That was not what Roy was now climbing up a ladder to get into.

"You've got to be kidding me," Albert murmured, mostly to himself.

Now at the top of the stairs and looping a leg over into the cockpit, Roy beamed a smile down at him.

"I've always wanted to fly one of these."

Albert almost choked.

"You've never flown one before?"

Roy frowned. "Of course not, old boy. These things went out of service decades before I joined the service. Only rich boys like Digger can afford one."

"Yes," remarked Digger. "Please be sure to bring it back in one piece."

If Albert's eyes had gone any wider, his eyeballs would have fallen clean out of his head. He was staring at a spitfire. Roy was sitting in the cockpit of a second world war fighter plane and expecting him to get in the back with Rex.

"I thought these were one-man things," he questioned, stalling for time.

The engine sputtered to life and the propeller spun.

Digger had to shout to make himself heard.

"They were, but converting them to seat two people is easy enough. It's how I made my money, old chap. I flew people in them. Giving them an experience only serious money can buy. You're in a hurry, yes?" Digger prompted, clearly expecting Albert to get in the plane.

Rex looked up at his human.

"We're getting in that?" he asked. He held none of the trepidation Albert felt, to Rex a mode of human transport was a mode of human transport. In the last few weeks alone he'd travelled on trains, buses, boats, and many, many cars. A plane was just another thing with wheels.

The stairs were steep, but no challenge for Rex. Getting into the plane was another thing entirely.

Albert clambered around him and once settled into the plane's backseat, had to heave/wrestle Rex until he reversed into the seat. There wasn't enough room for him to go between Albert's feet so as Roy increased the throttle and the aircraft began to move forward, Rex sat himself on Albert's lap.

In the cramped confines of the cockpit, Albert had Rex panting directly into his face, but that was the least of his worries. He was giving very serious consideration to changing his mind about trying to catch the Gastrothief's agents. Stopping criminals who needed to be stopped all sounded very noble until one had to risk dying in a tumbling fireball because one's neighbour lost control of the eighty-year-old fighter plane one had foolishly clambered into.

Too late, Roy gunned the throttle and the famous plane whipped down the grass runway at a terrific rate of knots. Pressed back into his seat, and slowly being crushed by Rex's weight, Albert let out a wail of panic.

The plane lifted into the air, the sensation of being airborne doing nothing for Albert's nerves.

Rex, sensing his human was upset, gave him a comforting lick.

"Arrrgh!" Albert protested.

Shouting to be heard over the engine noise, Roy asked, "Everything all right, old boy?"

Albert wiped his mouth. "Yes. It's all just peachy. Rex licked my teeth is all."

Roy shouted. "Sorry. Having trouble hearing you. Just hold on, I'm trying to figure out how to retract the landing gear."

Albert said some words Petunia would not have liked and closed his eyes. He stayed that way for the next fifteen minutes, trying to convince himself that the worst part was over even though he suspected the landing was where they were most likely to explode.

He would have kept his eyes closed for longer, but he detected a background noise coming through his headset and had to figure out where it was coming from.

Scrunching his face as Albert realised he recognised what he was hearing, he asked, "Are you humming the theme to Dick Barton?"

Roy boomed, "Yes! The Devil's Gallop. They don't make tunes like that anymore!" He went back to humming the tune, but at a higher volume and Albert found himself joining in. The two men belted out the old music from the Dick Barton radio show and though they were off key and a little tuneless, the pace of the music and the imagery it conjured was enough to scare away the fear gripping Albert's belly.

Until Roy stopped humming and shouted, "Coming in to land now."

Albert turned his head to the side, daring to look out and down. They were flying far closer to the ground than he expected, the streets and houses beneath him quite distinct. Now that he was looking, he realised he recognised features. The M2 motorway was just to their right. Or is that port on an aircraft? Albert didn't know and decided he didn't care.

They had made incredible time, the old plane equalling their efforts in proving that age is just a number.

Roy banked the plane, chattering into his headset as he communicated with Rochester airport's control tower.

The plane dropped lower; the terror Albert felt ratcheting up another notch. He held Rex as tightly as he could and prayed for what he honestly believed would be a miracle.

The seconds ticked by, and the plane plunged again, Albert's stomach rebelling enough to make him glad it was empty.

His eyes were pressed tightly shut once more so it came as a great surprise when he heard the engine noise change. His eyelids shot open, his heart taking a break from normal service because he believed the engine had just stopped working right when they were about to land.

He could not have been more wrong.

They were already on the ground. Roy had landed so smoothly that Albert hadn't even noticed.

Rex could see that they were on the ground too. He was indifferent about most forms of human transport, generally preferring his own legs. But if forced to give feedback, he would tell everyone that he didn't like flying. It was too cramped for a start.

Roy taxied between two small aircraft and reduced the throttle to idle speed.

Twisting his torso as far as it would go, he smiled at Albert and gave him a wave.

"How was that, old boy?"

Albert had a list of adjectives to employ, but chose to give his friend a wordless thumbs up instead. Through the glass of the cockpit, Albert could see someone approaching them at a jog. Whoever it was had a torch in their right hand and when they got closer, Albert could see it was a young man in his late twenties or early thirties.

He collected a set of stairs and brought them to the side of the spitfire.

Roy opened the cockpit and stood up. Raising both his arms like a prize fighter, he leaned his head to the left and then the right as he kissed his biceps.

"Wing Commander Hope?" enquired the young man as he positioned the mobile stairs. "Grandad said to expect you."

That he was Digger's grandson should have come as no surprise, but it did. In the course of his British culinary odyssey Albert had encountered several people who had become his companion for a spell, but none had felt as natural or as capable as Roy. What he'd been able to add in value just in the last few hours set him apart from everyone else.

Digger's grandson went by the name Hudson. He was a fifth-generation flyer, but more importantly he had a car and when Roy produced his phone and found Camilla had sent them Leon's address in a text message, Hudson knew precisely where it was.

With aching joints and protesting muscles, the bruised and battered men scurried after Hudson to get to his car. It was on the other side of the hanger, and they were running against the clock still.

If they dawdled now, all the effort to get to this point would have been in vain. An hour had elapsed – enough time for someone to have driven from Whitstable to Rochester. They had the final short leg of their journey to complete, and only then would they find out if Albert's hunch was right or wrong.

30

LEON HAROLD'S HOUSE

Mercifully, given the state of Rex's muddy coat, and how much of it Albert now had plastered to his clothing, Hudson's car wasn't an elegant Jaguar with a plush interior. It was a tricked-out Land Rover Defender with wipe-clean seats and a load compartment at the back that clearly got used for animal feed and such.

Rex went in the back, Hudson running ahead to drop the tail-gate so Rex could jump in. Less than five minutes after the wheels of the spitfire touched down, they were on their way to Leon Harold's house.

"Thank you for doing this, Hudson," Albert made a point of showing his appreciation. The young fellow was putting himself out for people he didn't know and doing so without complaint.

Albert got a nod of acknowledgement from Hudson but nothing more; the young man's attention was on the road as he left the airfield to join a deserted road leading through a small industrial estate.

When he did speak, it was to say, "The place you want is just around the next corner. What's this about anyway?"

Digger obviously hadn't passed on what Roy told him and Albert knew there wasn't enough time for a lengthy explanation.

"Some bad people are up to no good," he stated simply. "We believe we can intercept them and prevent a crime from occurring."

Hudson frowned. "Isn't that what the police are for?"

Albert nodded his head sadly. "Indeed. Unfortunately, I might be one hundred percent wrong about their target and I am already in a spot of bother for wasting their time with my previous guesses."

Hudson flicked his indicator and began to slow his car.

Sitting in the back seat with Roy in the front, Albert reached through to touch Hudson's shoulder.

"Stop here, please."

Hudson flicked his eyes up to the rear-view mirror to check Albert was serious.

"You don't want me to go in?" he asked. They were stopped in the road, indicating their intention to cross the other lane to reach the driveway of Leon Harold's house. It was a big place set right back from the road, and there were lights on inside to show there was someone home.

Albert undid his seat belt. "No. We'll go on foot from here. You've done enough already. If you want to leave us here, that's fine."

Hudson twisted in his seat to look at both Roy and Albert as Roy unclipped his seatbelt too. Rex was on his feet in the load compartment, wagging his tail and ready to go, for that was clearly what his human was about to do.

"What is going on?" Hudson frowned at them. "Grandad called me less than an hour ago and begged me to get here to meet his spitfire. All he told me was that two heroes needed my help, and I should assist them in any way I could. He didn't go into any more detail than that, and I didn't ask. I'm asking now though. I'm coming with you – that's what grandad would expect, but I'd be happier if I knew what I was getting into."

Albert might have refused help from another person, but there was something about Hudson that instilled a sense of confidence. He was tall and broad at the shoulder. He looked fit and capable and … well, it would be nice to have some young muscle around not least because Albert was feeling really rather weary.

Jabbing a finger up the road, Albert said, "Pull in up there. We'll explain better on the way."

Hudson did just that, parking his car on a grass verge and listening intently to the two old men as they regaled him with a tale too fanciful to be true. He believed it, nevertheless, because here they were attempting to stop a kidnapping.

"You think they might already be here?" Hudson asked. The three men, led by Rex, had entered the grounds of Leon Harold's house and were halfway down the driveway. It was dark, but any second now they expected to trip security lights as they neared the house.

Albert pulled a face that no one saw. "They might have been and gone. There's just no way to know until we get there."

"So … what? We knock on the door?" Hudson asked.

There were two cars parked in front of a double garage to the left of the house. Were they both Leon's? They could be. Or one could belong to Tanya and Baldwin. If they were here and Albert rang the front doorbell, it would destroy any chance he had of surprising them. If they were not here, then they were about to be, and he couldn't dawdle.

Albert dearly wanted to dial three nines and get the police moving in his direction. If he anonymously reported a break in or a crime in progress at their current address, the police would come, but he chose to wait, giving himself a few minutes to figure out if Leon was inside and safe, or already kidnapped. A different person might have acted otherwise, but Albert's long history as a police officer meant he knew only too well what it was like to have resources wasted unnecessarily.

Albert hated how much of a dilemma saving a man had become.

He needed to get a look inside and told his companions as much. If they looked through a window and saw Leon watching TV or having dinner, they could relax and hide in the shadows waiting to see if the Gastrothief's people showed up. If they were already here, or had clearly done the deed and left already, they could call the police and at least Albert would be able to prove the claims he made to Chief Inspector Quinn were true.

Rex listened to the humans talking and despaired. The people he chased in Whitstable, twice now in two days, were not here. Anyone could smell that. They hadn't been here at any point, but a man they met this morning was.

Rex sniffed deeply again, checking what he already knew to be true and yipped for attention. His human didn't even stop talking, he just reached down with one hand to ruffle the fur on Rex's head.

Rex yipped again, this time more insistently.

Albert, Roy, and Hudson had just decided to split up. Hudson would stay at the front of the house, out of sight in the shadow of a tree while Roy and Albert approached the house.

"What is it, Rex?" Albert looked down at his dog. "Can you smell something?"

Rex performed the canine equivalent of rolling his eyes.

"I can smell everything, dummy. The humans you want to catch are not here. Another one is. This is his home – it stinks of him. We don't need to sneak around looking, I can tell you what you need to know."

Albert said, "Shhhhh," a finger to his lips as he begged Rex to make less noise.

Rex made several uncharitable comments about Albert's mother and what she might have liked to do with Rottweilers in alleys. His noises were misinterpreted yet again as Albert did his best to translate them.

"Yes, boy, we're going to see if the man who lives here is home or not."

Albert set off, keeping to the edge of the front garden as he made his way toward the house. Roy was already there, peering around the edge of a window at the front of the house.

He whispered, "No sign of life," when Albert passed him.

Together they passed the front door to look in the windows on the other side and got the same result. If Leon was home, then he had to be in the back half of the property.

Rex muttered under his breath, but went with the humans when they snuck around the side of the house and through a gate to access the back garden.

No sooner did they get to the rear of the house than they saw the flickering light of a television playing inside. It meant Leon had been here, but nothing more than that – they had to get closer yet.

Rex tensed as Albert and Roy crept forward. A security light flicked on above their heads, bathing them in bright light.

The men froze to the spot, expecting a shout of outrage from inside the house, but what they heard next was a doorbell.

Rex's hackle slowly lifted, and he began to growl.

"They are here," he announced and would have started barking had Albert not been so swift to grab Rex's muzzle. "They're here," Rex mumbled nasally to his human who had crouched to make eye contact and was imploring his dog to keep quiet.

Still peering into the house, Roy reported, "Movement."

Albert twisted his head in time to see Leon Harold pass by a doorway inside the house. He was heading for the front door, going to find out who was there.

"Could it be them?" Roy asked, his voice filled with tension.

Frozen to the spot, and barely daring to breathe, they heard a man speak. Though his words were too indistinct to make out, when a cry of alarm rang out, it needed no translation.

Rex had already been poised to break free of his human's grip and the sound of panic was all he needed to gird him into action. He bucked, throwing his weight one way and then another. It was enough to knock Albert off balance, sending him to the damp grass as he fell.

Rex reversed direction, running back around the house to get to the front door.

Roy grabbed Albert's arm, hauling him from the ground as another shout came from within the house.

The backdoor to the house was three yards away and led into the kitchen. They ran for it, praying it would be unlocked and got there in time to see Leon Harold running through the house.

As Albert's hand closed around the door handle, something hit

Leon from behind. His arms went into the air as he spasmed and then pitched forward dead or unconscious.

Behind him, advancing down the house's central hallway were Tanya and Baldwin, the latter of which had just fired a taser gun. They looked confident and unflustered – just another day at the office, and a worrying thought crossed Albert's mind – what happened to Hudson?

31

UTTER BEDLAM

Albert ripped open the back door and piled through it with Roy on his heels. It startled Tanya and Baldwin who knew Leon Harold lived alone and thus were not expecting to find anyone else at the property.

However, the surprise they felt lasted for no more than the time it took to blink. Then they both smiled – the last piece of the puzzle had come to them. They would have fun extracting information from Albert Smith. He would reveal how it was that he knew where they were going to be and when the earl was done with him, he would be a satisfying kill.

"Two for one," grinned Baldwin, aiming a smile at Tanya.

Albert had come to a stop just inside the kitchen. Faced with two stone cold killers, it had abruptly dawned on him that he had no back up, no one was coming to their rescue because there had been no time to call the police, and he had no weapons he could employ to save himself or Leon Harold.

Roy stepped around his neighbour, gripping his walking cane in both hands.

"I'll take it from here, old boy," he quipped, giving the two ends of his cane a yank. They parted, a thin rapier sword emerging from within the cane.

Baldwin gave the old man an impressed nod of approval.

"Nice accessory. I'll add it to my collection."

Advancing, Roy gave the sword a swish, the blade parting the air in front of his face with a razor-sharp sounding whoosh.

"I used to fence for Oxford, young man."

Baldwin shrugged and took out his gun.

"I used to kill people for the British Secret Service," he replied, levelling the gun at Roy's head.

Roy said, "Ah," and raised his hands.

Albert did likewise, but also started talking.

"There's something rather important the two of you have overlooked," he remarked cryptically.

Baldwin sniggered, questioning whether he should shoot the old man with the sword and get it over with – they didn't need him – or choose a quieter method of dispatch.

"Oh, yes?" he asked, deciding that it had been a while since he strangled anyone. "And what is that?"

Two yards behind him, something had been bothering Tanya ever since the old men burst through the kitchen door. Only now that Albert had asked the question did she realise what it was.

"Where's his dog!" she blurted, just as the sound of thundering paws hit the carpet behind her.

Rex put his head down and ploughed through Tanya's legs. Striking the meaty part of her left thigh with his skull as she turned toward him, he blasted the petite woman into the air. She hung at the apex of her upward trajectory for a nanosecond before gravity reclaimed her, but by then Rex had run beneath her flailing body and was leaping at Baldwin.

In a moment of uncharacteristic panic, Baldwin's gun went off, the unaimed round finding a target anyway.

Roy yelled in pain and fell backward.

It happened at the same time as Rex piled into Baldwin's back. The German Shepherd dog weighed less than half of his target, but his momentum and the violence of his attack were sufficient to bear Baldwin to the floor.

The gun went off again, a second unaimed shot putting a hole in Leon's skirting board.

Rex bit into the flesh of Baldwin's right arm, drawing a scream of agony and forcing him to drop the gun.

Albert caught Roy before he could fall, lowering him gently to the kitchen tile next to the back door. It was a scene of utter bedlam, the echoes of the most recent shot still reverberating in Albert's ears while Tanya crashed back down to the hallway carpet in a tangle of limbs and Rex did his best to rip off Baldwin's arm.

Baldwin yelled for help, cursing and squealing in equal measure. He didn't stop fighting though, swinging his left fist like a club as he tried to free his arm from the dog's jaws.

"I'm fine," gasped Roy through clenched teeth. The bullet had gouged a hole in his coat and carved a path through the skin of his left shoulder. It was bleeding plenty and it hurt, but he knew it wasn't life-threatening. "Get them for me, Albert!"

Albert spun away from his friend, grabbing Roy's sword, and looking up just in time to see Tanya aim a taser at Rex.

The electrodes hit the German Shepherd in the rump, discharging a non-lethal charge instantly.

Rex spasmed, but so too did Baldwin who caught as much of the stunning voltage as the dog.

Both stopped fighting and though neither lost consciousness, they were not about to get up. With Roy out of the picture and no sign of Hudson, it left just Albert and Tanya.

She was sitting on the hallway carpet looking like she was injured if the grimace of pain on her face was any indication.

Albert got to watch as she shifted her legs around to get up and reached inside her jacket. His eyes flared when he realised she was going for a gun of her own and he darted forward to grab Baldwin's abandoned weapon.

He'd never been one for guns. In his day very few criminals had them and the police ran around with truncheons. Now faced with no choice, he aimed the gun at Tanya just as she brought hers to bear on him.

Through gritted teeth, she said, "I'm not going to shoot you, Albert and I want you to not shoot me."

It was a classic standoff, neither party holding any advantage. They were five yards apart and if one shot first the other would pull their trigger automatically. At such a short distance the likelihood of missing was minimal, and Tanya was not prepared to risk it even though she doubted Albert would shoot first.

"I'm going to take my partner and leave," she announced calmly. "You win this round."

Her comment seemed like an odd thing to say, but now that he had her talking, he had questions of his own.

"What is all this about, Tanya?"

She almost asked how he could possibly know her name, but caught herself before she did. Forcing a smile onto her lips, she said, "You give yourself away, Albert. I thought you knew everything, and it had me genuinely worried. Now I learn that you are just chasing shadows." Keeping the gun trained on Albert's centre of mass, she stood up.

Albert saw her wince, but his hope that she might be too injured to leave evaporated.

"Back up," she commanded. "I'm taking my partner. If you try to stop me or I think you are going to try something stupid, I will start shooting and none of us will get to walk out of here tonight."

Albert believed her.

Baldwin was a dead weight, especially since Tanya was attempting to drag him over the kitchen tile using only one hand. The other held the gun and her eyes never once left Albert's face.

She used a boot to push Rex to one side. He was panting and his eyes were open, but other than lifting his head, he made no attempt to get up.

Baldwin was stirring too, and a good thing too because there was no chance Tanya would have been able to drag him over the far greater friction offered by the hallway carpet.

"Come on," Tanya insisted. "On your feet."

Groggy and disorientated, Baldwin managed to get his feet under his body and with Tanya's help, he managed to get upright. It was then that Albert got to see just how much blood Baldwin was losing. Rex's teeth must have found the artery in his arm because there was a smeared pool of it under where his body had been lying and now it was dripping steadily from his fingertips.

Tanya backed Baldwin to the front door and stepped outside. A glance over her shoulder as she did was the first time she had taken her eyes off Albert since the stalemate began. He could have pulled his trigger right then – she had handed him the opportunity. He could stop them and finally get some answers, but in the space between heartbeats when he questioned whether he should, she was gone.

No one said anything and precious seconds ticked by. When a car's engine started up, it sent a spark through Albert, and he ran for the front door. He was going to call the police in the next few seconds and giving them the number plate for the car Tanya was driving would help them immensely.

However, the moment he stuck his head outside, Tanya shot at him. The bullet struck the plaster right by his head – she had been aiming to kill him.

The car reversed at speed onto the street and spun around. The driver's window was open; Albert could see it from his position flat on the hallway carpet.

"Rules, Albert," Tanya shouted. "There are rules."

32

ON THE RUN

A squeal of tyres left a trail of rubber on the road and the car was gone. Albert levered himself off the floor, made sure the gun's safety was on and dumped it in a coat pocket. He was the only one left standing.

He felt like warmed up death, but Rex, Roy, and Hudson all needed his help.

When he turned to look back down the hallway to the kitchen, he found Roy kneeling next to Rex. Rex was licking Roy's hand and though Albert was still concerned about both of them, he needed to find out what had happened to Hudson first.

He announced his intention and got a wave from Roy.

"You go on, old boy. We're all good in here. I might need to wake that Leon chap up though. I could do with a brandy."

Albert asked his neighbour to call the police and went outside to search the front garden.

Hudson was exactly where they had left him. Well, not exactly, I suppose. When they left him, he was upright, now he was flat on the dirt in a flowerbed with a cracker of a lump on the side of his skull.

He roused when Albert touched his shoulder, complaining that his head felt like someone was running around inside it with a chainsaw.

By the time they got back inside Roy was resting on Leon's couch with a brandy in his hand. Leon had one too though his was untouched and being eyed up by Roy who felt quite certain this was not a one drink situation. Beverly was on her way, coming to collect her husband and take him home.

Her reaction to his brief account of the evening events was to shout and get tearful before professing her love and insisting she would never again let him out of her sight.

Rex was hungry. Hungry enough that no other emotion or thought could find its way into his head. There was an itchy patch on his back end which he'd been worrying with his teeth to no benefit. It was where the electrodes had left a slight burn to his skin, but he had no other injuries. He was on the couch too, lying with his jaw on Roy's right thigh.

It was testament to how bewildered Leon Harold was that he'd not even noticed the trail of crumbling mud the dog was leaving everywhere in his perfectly pristine home.

In an armchair on the other side of the room, Hudson sat quietly with his eyes closed and a bag of frozen peas on his skull.

Albert had been listening for the police to arrive and went outside when he heard a siren approaching. It had taken them less than ten minutes, a single squad car arriving at speed with a short black woman at the wheel and a terrified white guy in the seat next to her.

The male cop was complaining to his partner.

"I know I said to get there fast, Patience, but I wanted to arrive in one piece."

The short black woman gave him a deep frown. "You are in one piece, Brad. If you want to complain about my driving, do it yourself."

Brad threw his arms in the air. "I tried, Patience. You got in first and wouldn't get out."

"That's because I like to drive sometimes, you chauvinist pig!"

Two yards from the front door, she dropped her frown and smiled at Albert. "Hello, Sir. Are you the one who put in the call?"

"Sort of," he replied, backing inside and leading them to find everyone else.

An ambulance peeled into the driveway before the cops could get into the house and Constable Brad Hardacre went to deal with it.

More cops arrived after the paramedics and not so very long after that, Albert's daughter, Selina appeared. She flashed her police identification and found her dad in the lounge along with Rex, Roy, Hudson, Leon, and everyone else who had already arrived.

Albert lifted a tired arm to wave at her and let her know he was all right.

She came to kneel next to him, leaning in close to whisper.

"Are you okay, Dad?"

"Tired, love, and a little battered. I have had quite a day."

Selina absorbed his report and pressed on, whispering so no one else would hear.

"There is a warrant out for your arrest. Have you told anyone your name?"

Albert shook his head. "No, love. I suspected there might be. That Chief Inspector Quinn can be quite tetchy."

Selina grimaced. "Yes, he's been on the phone to my boss already. The Commissioner is getting involved in person. Gary is trying to smooth things over, but we are going to have to come clean about the misappropriated resources we have employed to help you investigate the Gastrothief. If we don't get in front of this, it could end all our careers."

Albert gritted his teeth. He felt like cursing. The Gastrothief was real – tonight's escapade stood as a perfect demonstration that Albert was right, yet he had to fight uphill against bureaucratic idiots like Chief Inspector Quinn.

"You can't go home, Dad. What are you going to do? If you want to face this head on, I can take you into custody myself."

Selina's offer shocked Albert for a second, but as the concept filtered into his head, he saw the sense in it. He could defuse Quinn's attack and with the statements Hudson, Roy, and Leon would give, they could create enough doubt that Gary, Selina, and Albert's youngest, Randall, would be given the opportunity to prove the case.

Despite that, he shook his head. There was something he hadn't told the police. He hadn't told Roy either. Once he'd settled people in the lounge, he went to fetch brandy glasses from a kitchen cupboard. Tiptoeing to get around the blood, his foot struck something, and he looked down to find a phone.

There was blood on it, but one swipe of the screen was all it took to know it had fallen from Baldwin's pocket. Standing in the kitchen in the period before the police arrived, he'd opened the message, call, and email apps, quickly looking through them because those were things he knew how to do.

There were hundreds of calls and emails and messages, and it would take him hours to go through them, but one email had stuck out, his eyes drawn to it the moment he saw who it was from. It was for a hotel reservation in Cornwall and the date of the booking was two days from now.

Baldwin wasn't going, his injuries would preclude him, but someone else might. They might be with Tanya, or it might be Tanya by herself. Or it could be a completely different team just like in Biggleswade. The who didn't matter because Albert knew it would be someone.

They might even change the date of their arrival given that Baldwin wouldn't be able to go, but Albert could wait. He knew he would need to be clever with credit cards and such, but he had a plan for how he would stay under the radar.

The point was that he couldn't afford to be arrested and processed and messed around while the powers that be tried to decide if there really was a master criminal at work. They wouldn't keep him in a cell. In fact, Albert believed he would be home within hours unless they kept him in for multiple rounds of questioning.

It was too risky though.

He explained as much to Selina, leaving out the part about having a destination in mind.

"Where will you go, Dad?" she asked.

"Tonight? Home to grab some things and then to a hotel nearby. If I don't tell you, you won't have to lie."

Selina nodded her head, slowly and regretfully. Her father was brave and resourceful and above all he was a great detective. If anyone could follow the Gastrothief's trail and catch him, it was her dad. She wanted to tell him not to, but she already knew he wouldn't listen. The only way she could prevent him from pursuing the case now was by arresting him, and she couldn't do that. Not in a million years.

She stood up, announcing her intention to take her father home, and leaving her details with a uniformed sergeant who was the current senior member of the local police at the scene.

Rex leapt off the couch when Albert asked if he wanted his dinner. Roy's shoulder had been patched up and Beverly was due to arrive at any minute.

Albert made a point of shaking his friend's hand before he left.

"Thank you, Roy. I needed you today."

"Together to the end, old boy. Just like I said." A moment of silence passed between them before Roy added, "Listen, old chum, I've been thinking about taking a trip back to my old stomping grounds in Europe. I was stationed there at different RAF bases for most of my career. I'll be too old for it if I don't go soon. I was wondering if you might fancy another trip at some point in the future?"

A smile split Albert's face – it was a fun notion. It wasn't for him to consider now though – he had bigger fish to fry. He left Roy with a promise to discuss it at greater length when he was done touring Great Britain.

In Selina's car on the way home, Albert realised he didn't have anything much to eat in his house. His fridge was empty, and he was far too tired to start defrosting and cooking anything he might find in his freezer. Also, he needed to get in and out quickly.

So for the third time in two days, he stopped off for fish and chips and sat on the back seat of his daughter's car sharing them with Rex as she took him home.

33

SHALLOW GRAVE

Tanya buried Baldwin's body in a shallow grave in the new forest. He could have survived his injuries if taken directly to a hospital, but that was never an option. It wasn't so much the fact that the police might find him there, Tanya saw his wound as an opportunity to remove a thorn in her side.

The earl could give her a new partner or send her out alone, she really didn't care which so long as she wasn't stuck with Baldwin and his annoying advances any longer.

His death gave her a scapegoat for the Albert Smith problem too. Yes, Albert got away, but that's because Baldwin was careless. *Don't worry, Earl, I made sure to cover our tracks. How are the oysters?*

She could see it all in her head. The earl would buy her version of events and it wasn't as if there was anyone to dispute them.

Her leg hurt where the dog had hit it, but it was nothing more than bruising. She would limp for a few days most likely, but no worse than that.

Halfway back to the earl's lair, she found a new car to steal and set the previous one ablaze. Her stupid fake identification with the ridiculous name went up in flames with it. Duke Ironhammer was dead and so too was Lisa Delicious.

Swallowing a couple of painkillers with some coffee that had gone cold more than an hour ago, she settled back behind the steering wheel and turned her thoughts to Cornwall. That was her next destination unless the earl saw fit to change her travel plans, and she rather liked that part of the world.

EPILOGUE

Albert awoke to the sound of Rex panting in his face. As his eyelids fluttered open and Rex tried to lick his eyeballs, Albert scooted back across the bed to escape.

"I need to go out," Rex announced, dancing over to the door and looking at it meaningfully.

Albert understood the message well enough.

"I'm up. I'm up," he sighed, swinging his legs out of bed. A yawn split his head in two and kept going for long enough that he started to think he might have to push his bottom jaw shut. When finally it subsided, Albert stood up, crossing the room to find his coat and shoes while scratching himself liberally all over.

They were staying in a luxury country spa just a few miles from his house. It was the sort of place that hosted big parties and plush weddings. For Albert it was just somewhere to lie low for a day or so.

Roy had booked it for him without question or hesitation the previous evening and a taxi had delivered Albert and Rex in time for last orders at the bar. Not that Albert had visited the bar. He was keeping his head down and planning to talk to as few people as he could get away with.

Rex still needed to go out though.

Albert moved slowly, his body protesting from the bruises it sported - there were too many to count. It was early in the morning, too early for most guests to be awake in Albert's opinion, so he didn't bother to clip Rex's lead. The last thing Albert needed right now was his dog yanking his arms about – they hurt too much.

At the door to the grounds, Albert let Rex run off, calling after him to not go too far. Then he found a bench to sit on, resting his weary body while Rex sniffed and snuffled and picked his spot.

Sitting on another bench just a few yards along from him was a young woman in her late teens. She was wearing sports clothing and had the look about her of a person who actually played sports rather than someone who wore the gear because it was comfortable.

He corrected his assessment a moment later when he saw her idly swinging a set of nunchucks from one hand: she was a martial artist, not a sportswoman.

Rex was oblivious to the young woman with the nunchucks; he was following the scent of a bulldog. Not for any reason other than for something to do, but when he stopped to sniff at a tree the bulldog had marked, the dog in question appeared.

"Here for the wedding then?" The bulldog asked.

Rex tilted his head to one side. "No. I don't think so. My human didn't say anything about a wedding. Is that what you are here for?"

"Sort of. My human, Felicity, is the one running it. It's what she does. I'm Buster by the way, although," Buster leaned in close so he could whisper conspiratorially, "I do have a superhero name. They call me Devil Dog."

Rex raised his left eyebrow, and drawled, "Riiiiiight," as he questioned whether the bulldog might have hit his head recently.

"Anyway," Buster continued. "There are dozens of dogs coming to the wedding so I thought you might be one of them. The bride has a champion Pomeranian and … well, Felicity explained it, but it was long and boring, and I fell asleep before she finished. The point is there are lots of dogs here."

Rex had wondered why he'd been able to smell so many different dogs when they arrived last night. Now he knew.

"Buster!"

At the sound of his name being called, the bulldog swung around to look back at the hotel.

"That's Mindy," he explained. "She works for Felicity."

Mindy called, "Come on, Buster. I want some breakfast."

Trotting away, Buster said, "See you around ... I didn't get your name."

"Rex," said Rex. "See you around." He went back to sniffing the tree not giving a moment's thought to whether his statement might prove true or not.

The End

Except, as usual, it isn't. Rex and Albert will be back soon in **_Wedding Ceremony Woes_**, a Felicity Philips Investigates story. This will be just a brief interlude in their journey, of course, brought about by mutual geography. Soon enough, your favourite man and dog duo will arrive at their next destination, and it will not be long before they reach the pulse-pounding climax of this series.

BONUS CHAPTER

If you cannot wait, and you are thirsty for more, there's a bonus chapter waiting for you right now. Click the link below or copy it into your web browser.
https://stevehiggsbooks.com/rexs-garden-invasion/

34

AUTHOR'S NOTE

Dear Reader,
Thank you for being interested enough to read the author's waffling nonsense at the back of the book. I could easily prattle on for days about how grateful I am that anyone buys my books, but I have grown to accept that (for whatever reason) I write stories that people like.

I have enormous fun crafting these tales, gladly staying up into the small hours to get my thoughts onto the page most weeks if not most days.

If you read the dedication right at the start, you might be questioning what that is all about. If you haven't read it, go back and do so now. I'll wait.

Ready?

In the current climate of social distancing, health above all else, and governments imposing heavy tax on alcohol, it is a brave man who goes into business as a publican. I don't know Tim the landlord other than to exchange pleasantries when I enter his establishment, yet I feel a certain kindred spirit exists.

He has transformed the village pub from a shabby space that attracted lager boys and the Sunday football crowd to a refined and attractive space where couples and families dine and converse. I believe such an accomplishment to be no easy feat.

In this book I write about Earl Bacon chowing on some delicacies. My research showed me that some of the items I listed in his meal are among the most expensive on earth. Of course, the character I have created would want them purely because of their cost.

Porker sausages are not a real thing. There is a famous and readily available sausage made by a firm with a similar name and they may or may not have a place of business in Reculver. I like eating sausages, I always have. I guess that is due to taste and variety though it could easily be just because my dad liked them and as a boy I liked whatever my dad liked – he was my world.

I mention two Dicks in this book – Dick Turpin and Dick Barton. If you are not familiar with either, then you are not British, and their notoriety is less widespread than I hoped.

Dick Turpin is a famous highwayman – a person who robbed you at gunpoint in the 18th century. His short life of crime is one which has been romanticised ever since, most notably for the author in a television series in the late seventies.

Dick Barton is a sleuth, adventurer, and all-around precursor to the likes of Indiana Jones and the Marvel superheroes as he defeated bad guys aplenty with his sidekicks along to lend a hand. A famous radio show in the late forties, it made it to the screen when Hammer made three movies which at the time of writing can be seen via Amazon Prime.

His theme tune, The Devil's Gallop, is a fun romp that looks jolly hard for anyone but a skilled musician to even attempt. To me it stands as a fine example of a composer capturing the essence of action in their notes.

In this book I make a comment about airport parking prices costing more than the flights. This is based on my experience and is no exaggeration. Flight prices have dropped and dropped, almost to the point that they are stupidly cheap. Many years ago, when my wife and I were still dating and I was stationed in north Germany, I booked her a series of flights to visit me for my birthday and then Christmas and all for less than the price of dinner out.

I more recently parked at Stanstead airport, one of the smaller airports servicing London and the cost of leaving my car overnight was greater than a return trip to Prague.

I think that's about enough waffling from me. I'm glad you enjoyed the book, I'm off to write another.

Take care.

Steve Higgs

WHAT'S NEXT FOR ALBERT AND REX

When the chef tipped to win this year's annual Eton Mess competition goes missing, Albert races to investigate - surely this is the work of the Gastrothief again.

However, Albert barely makes it out of the train station before his detective's brain sees something most other people would never spot – a crime is about to take place and there's no way he can ignore it. Instantly shackled with a new problem, Albert attempts to solve both cases simultaneously, but is he up to the task?

It's a good thing he has trusted partner Rex Harrison, the oversized former police dog, ready to lend a paw because this time he's going to need all the help he can get.

New sidekicks to meet, new dishes to taste, and yet another deadly adventure await as Albert and Rex try to give the bad guys their just desserts!

RECIPE

Oysters could be considered an ingredient or a dish in their own right, and I see them more commonly served over ice in their raw form with just a dressing to add flavour. However, to provide the recipe hungry readers that I know my books reach, I chose to select a dish that includes oysters as a feature rather than the main attraction. I also picked it because I know Albert and Rex would both approve.

Beef and Oyster Pie

Beef and oyster pie is a classic Victorian dish, it was the food of the poor and the poorer you were the more oysters you would put in your pie. Oysters were plentiful, the smaller ones sold as fast food on the streets of London or pickled to keep, while the bigger ones were put in stews and pies.

Ingredients

- 900g/2lb stewing beef, trimmed, cut into rough 3cm/1¼in cubes
- 2-3 tbsp sunflower oil
- 3 long shallots, quartered
- 2 garlic cloves, finely chopped

- 125g/4½oz smoked, rindless, streaky bacon rashers, cut into 1cm/½in strips
- 1 tbsp roughly chopped thyme leaves
- 2 bay leaves
- 330ml/11fl oz stout
- 400ml/14fl oz beef stock (made with one stock cube)
- flaked sea salt and freshly ground black pepper
- 2 tbsp cornflour, blended with 2 tbsp water to make a smooth paste
- 8 oysters, freshly shucked

For the pastry

- 400g/14oz plain flour, plus extra for rolling
- ¼ tsp salt
- 250g/9oz butter, frozen for at least 2 hours
- 1 free-range egg, beaten, to glaze

Method

1. Season the beef cubes with salt and black pepper. Heat a tablespoon of oil in the frying pan and fry the meat over a high heat. Do this in three batches so that you don't overcrowd the pan, transferring the meat to a large flameproof casserole dish once it is browned all over. Add extra oil if the pan seems dry.
2. In the same pan, add another tablespoon of oil and cook the shallots for 4-5 minutes, then add the garlic and fry for 30 seconds. Add the bacon and fry until slightly browned. Transfer the onion and bacon mixture to the casserole dish and add the herbs.
3. Preheat the oven to 180C/350F/Gas 4.
4. Pour the stout into the frying pan and bring to the boil, stirring to lift any stuck-on browned bits from the bottom of the pan. Pour the stout over the beef in the casserole dish and add the stock. Cover the casserole and place it

in the oven for 1½-2 hours, or until the beef is tender and the sauce is reduced.

5. Skim off any surface fat, taste and add salt and pepper if necessary, then stir in the cornflour paste. Put the casserole dish on the hob – don't forget that it will be hot – and simmer for 1-2 minutes, stirring, until thickened. Leave to cool.

6. Increase the oven to 200C/400F/Gas 6. To make the pastry, put the flour and salt in a very large bowl. Grate the butter and stir it into the flour in three batches. Gradually add 325ml/11fl oz cold water – you may not need it all – and stir with a round-bladed knife until the mixture just comes together. Knead the pastry lightly into a ball on a lightly floured surface and set aside 250g/9oz for the pie lid.

7. Roll the rest of the pastry out until about 2cm/¾in larger than the dish you're using. Line the dish with the pastry then pile in the filling, tucking the oysters in as well. Brush the edge of the pastry with beaten egg.

8. Roll the remaining pastry until slightly larger than your dish and gently lift over the filling, pressing the edges firmly to seal, then trim with a sharp knife. Brush with beaten egg to glaze. Put the dish on a baking tray and bake for 25-30 minutes, or until the pastry is golden-brown and the filling is bubbling.

MORE COZY MYSTERY

On board the world's finest luxury cruise ship, the days are filled with sunshine, cocktails, and incredible new places to explore.

Unless you are employed as the ship's detective, that is.

That job falls to a lady called Patricia Fisher, a whip-smart sleuth whose special skills include attracting trouble, getting shot at, and running away screaming.

So, when a mysterious stowaway is found murdered in the bowels of the ship, it falls firmly into her lap to work out not only who he is, but who killed him.

To a backdrop of petty thefts, con artists targeting the rich and famous on board, and her own romance with the captain, the dead body leads to a surprising discovery and a word one should utter with care …

Treasure.

Thrown into a swirling maelstrom of deadly adventure, fifty-something Patricia is going to have her sleuthing skills tested to the maximum.

Get ready for murder and mayhem on the high seas.

BLUE MOON INVESTIGATIONS

The paranormal? It's all nonsense but proving it might just get them all killed.

When a master vampire starts killing people in his hometown, paranormal investigator, Tempest Michaels, takes it personally ...

... and soon a race against time turns into a battle for his life.

He doesn't believe in the paranormal but has a steady stream of clients with cases too weird for the police to bother with. Mostly it's all nonsense, but when a third victim turns up with bite marks in her lifeless throat, can he really dismiss the possibility that this time the monster is real?

Joined by an ex-army buddy, a disillusioned cop, his friends from the pub, his dogs, and his mother (why are there no grandchildren, Tempest), our paranormal investigator is going to stop the murders if it kills him ...

... but when his probing draws the creature's attention, his family and friends become the hunted.

MORE BOOKS BY STEVE HIGGS

Blue Moon Investigations

Paranormal Nonsense

The Phantom of Barker Mill

Amanda Harper Paranormal Detective

The Klowns of Kent

Dead Pirates of Cawsand

In the Doodoo with Voodoo

The Witches of East Malling

Crop Circles, Cows and Crazy Aliens

Whispers in the Rigging

Bloodlust Blonde – a short story

Paws of the Yeti

Under a Blue Moon – A Paranormal Detective Origin Story

Night Work

Lord Hale's Monster

The Herne Bay Howlers

Undead Incorporated

The Ghoul of Christmas Past

The Sandman

Jailhouse Golem

Shadow in the Mine
Ghost Writer

Patricia Fisher Cruise Mysteries
The Missing Sapphire of Zangrabar
The Kidnapped Bride
The Director's Cut
The Couple in Cabin 2124
Doctor Death
Murder on the Dancefloor
Mission for the Maharaja
A Sleuth and her Dachshund in Athens
The Maltese Parrot
No Place Like Home
What Sam Knew
Solstice Goat
Recipe for Murder
A Banshee and a Bookshop
Diamonds, Dinner Jackets, and Death
Frozen Vengeance
Mug Shot
The Godmother
Murder is an Artform
Wonderful Weddings and Deadly Divorces
Dangerous Creatures
Patricia Fisher: Ship's Detective
Fitness Can Kill
Death by Pirates

Albert Smith Culinary Capers
Pork Pie Pandemonium
Bakewell Tart Bludgeoning
Stilton Slaughter
Bedfordshire Clanger Calamity
Death of a Yorkshire Pudding
Cumberland Sausage Shocker

Arbroath Smokie Slaying
Dundee Cake Dispatch
Lancashire Hotpot Peril
Blackpool Rock Bloodshed
Kent Coast Oyster Obliteration
Eton Mess Massacre

Felicity Philips Investigates

To Love and to Perish
Tying the Noose
Aisle Kill Him
A Dress to Die for
Wedding Ceremony Woes

Real of False Gods

Untethered magic
Unleashed Magic
Early Shift
Damaged but Powerful
Demon Bound
Familiar Territory
The Armour of God
Terrible Secrets
Top Dog
Hellfire Hellion

Printed in Great Britain
by Amazon

42051111R00129